THE

IRON CHARIOT

Stein Riverton

TRANSLATED FROM THE NORWEGIAN
BY
LUCY MOFFATT

Published by
Lightning Books Ltd
Imprint of EyeStorm Media
312 Uxbridge Road
Rickmansworth
Hertfordshire
WD3 8YL

www.lightning-books.com

First published as *Jernvognen* in Norway in 1909
Translation copyright © 2017 by Lucy Moffatt
This translation first published by Abandoned Bookshop in 2017

Cover design by Ifan Bates

British Library Cataloguing in Publication Data
A catalogue record for this book is available from the British Library

Printed by CPI Group (UK) Ltd, Croydon CR0 4YY

ISBN 9781785631610

Introduction

STEIN RIVERTON WAS THE PEN NAME of Norwegian journalist and author, Sven Elvestad (1884-1934). Born Kristoffer Elvestad Svendsen in the small south-eastern town of Halden, he grew up in straitened circumstances thanks to the fecklessness of his father, a sea captain who squandered his wages on drink and womanising.

Elvestad's literary potential was evident from an early age: he wrote his first story at 12 and was encouraged in his ambitions by a teacher. But when his father died in a shipwreck in 1900 – an event that would mark his son for life – the family was thrown into penury, and Elvestad, then 15, had to help support them by working for a timber merchant in Kristiania (now Oslo).

It was at this point that he first embarked on his journalistic career, writing on the side for papers in his hometown under the name of Sven Elvestad. Sacked from his day job for moonlighting, he returned to Halden, where he honed his craft working for local papers. He came to national attention in 1902 with an article in which he claimed to have solved the then-notorious Skjeberg murder, although his version of events turned out to be largely speculative. Shortly afterwards, according to his biographer Bernt Rougthvedt, he over-egged a story about the bankruptcy of two minor companies in Halden, throwing the town's business community into turmoil, and the ensuing public condemnation nearly scuppered his career.

By late 1903 he was back in Kristiania, where he worked for a series of newspapers and made a name for himself with bold stunts such as interviewing a circus lion in its cage, spending two days on turbulent seas in a dubious new sea-rescue system and reporting a spaceship landing in the industrial town of Notodden – an April fool that provoked queues at railway stations and questions in parliament.

He also gained a reputation as a fine stylist and gifted interviewer, eventually settling at *Tidens Tegn* newspaper, where he wrote articles, travelogues and interviews of exceptionally high quality until his death at 50. He also wrote a number of novels under the Elvestad name. Less admirable was his political stance: through the 1920s, Elvestad wrote articles in praise of Mussolini's Italy, and he was the first foreign journalist to interview Hitler in 1923 – although he appears to have been alarmed by the future Führer's brutality. As an article in Norway's cultural weekly, *Morgenbladet,* wryly noted when the Rougthvedt biography was published in 2007: '...it was probably good for his posthumous reputation that he died in 1934. There are grounds to assume that he would not have ended up on the right side.'

Elvestad turned his hand to crime writing in around 1904, anonymously penning serials for various newspapers. Two of

4

his creations proved especially enduring: Knut Gribb, a detective who first appeared in 1908, was passed on to other writers in 1909 and featured in a radio play as recently as 2010; and Asbjørn Krag, among the main reasons for Elvestad's continued fame. Elvestad adopted the pseudonym of Stein Riverton when Krag made his way into book form in 1907.

It is generally accepted that Elvestad/Riverton's hundred or so detective novels were variable in quality – hardly surprising considering the fiendish pace at which he wrote and his legendary alcohol intake – and opinion is divided over just how many still merit attention. His entry in the *Norwegian Biographical Lexicon* names nine; the introduction to a 2012 edition of *Morderen fra mørket (The Murderer from the Darkness)* names thirteen. But nobody disputes that *The Iron Chariot,* published in 1909, is his masterpiece.

According to Rougthvedt, Elvestad consciously set out to write a book that would combine suspense with literary quality, placing him among the masters in the genre. And he succeeded, creating a marvellously atmospheric tale of murder that may have echoes of Conan Doyle – there is even a ghostly dog! – but still achieves originality. This is largely thanks to the writing, which is richly descriptive and studded with striking imagery: a dog has a 'snout as round and black as the muzzle of a rifle'; a bank of clouds at sunset becomes 'a fantastical parade of astonishing beasts with fiery manes, embers sparking beneath their winged hooves'. As the book progresses, and the unnamed narrator becomes increasingly troubled by the sinister events around him, the imagery often serves to amplify his disturbed state of mind.

The temporal setting of the book plays an important role in creating its atmosphere, too. The almost unbearable brightness of midsummer at the opening of the novel inexorably yields to the darkness of approaching autumn, mirroring the detective's implacable progress towards the solution of the mystery.

The supernatural elements of the book are eerily effective, playing on common anxieties such as fear of the dark, of isolation, of being watched. The repeated image of the drowned man takes on added significance once we know that Elvestad's own father died at sea, seeming to suggest that the author has tapped into a very personal source of disquiet.

Thematically, the book reflects Elvestad's distrust of the modern and his vision of the detective story as a genre in tune with his own discordant age. The summer quiet is cut through by the pulse of motorboats; new technology (telegraph, telephone, fast trains and speedboats) intrudes upon a community still reliant on horse and carriage. The pastoral tranquillity of the island is interrupted by violence. And the iron chariot of the title, initially evoked in Old Testament-like terms, proves to be thoroughly modern. At the end of the novel, we are left with a sense that the narrator is relieved to be released from this chaotic world into 'stillness and silence'.

The novel's use of a narrative twist that another crime-writing great would later, more famously, deploy is perhaps not as effective as it would have been to its original readers in 1909. And yet the book still stands. Writer Nils Nordberg, an expert on crime fiction, put his finger on one reason why it remains so effective in a 2009 article in Norwegian daily, *Dagbladet*: 'The *Iron Chariot* was far ahead of its time…because the novel was something nobody had tried before: a psychological thriller disguised as a detective novel, with one foot in the horror tradition of Poe and the other in the modern world. It points towards much later writers such as Simenon, Patricia Highsmith and even Karin Fossum for that matter.'

Met on publication with comparisons to Conan Doyle and

even Dostoevsky, the novel has retained its appeal in Norway to this day, and has been regularly reprinted, most recently in 2015. It has been name-checked by many of the current crop of crime writers, including Jo Nesbø, Tom Egeland, Jørn Lier Horst and Kjell Ola Dahl. The Norwegian crime-writers' association, the Riverton Club – which is named after the author and also makes an annual crime fiction award called the Riverton Prize – voted it the best Norwegian crime novel of all time in 2017. A specialist jury ranked it second in *Dagbladet's* list of the twenty-five best Norwegian crime novels in 2009, while a public poll shortly afterwards placed it at number 16. If, as Nordberg also claims in the article cited above, *The Iron Chariot* is 'one of the best crime novels not just in Norway but the world', it deserves to find an equally wide and enthusiastic readership in the English-speaking world.

LUCY MOFFATT, TRANSLATOR

I

Three People Running

It was perhaps approaching eleven in the morning, and most of the summer guests at the boarding house had gradually drifted out after breakfast to set up camp on the grass in front of the veranda.

After several chilly days, the languorous heat of summer had finally arrived. It had rained in the night but the bad weather had cleared at around seven and the sun had then sparkled the whole morning through, drying the grass and soil, steaming away the puddles and baking the roads hard and white.

And now the summer guests rejoiced over the arrival at last of the great, driving summer, with its vast abundance of heat. And so they had laid themselves out in the baking sun, lay prostrate now, scattered in the high grass, squinting at the quivering light and lending an ear to the whisper out at sea. They listened for the summer breeze, which prised itself loose out in the ocean and glided over the rocky crests, penetrating the spruce forest, which sapped its feeble strength, and faltering over the meadows, where it barely managed to shake the grass and tickle the faces of the resting people.

From where I lay in the grass, I had a glimpse of a white muslin bodice, a woman's golden neck, hair slowly stirring; but if I turned my head a trifle, my gaze fell upon the hotel awning, its bright red stripes set in charming disarray by the play of the sunbeams.

Five people lay in the grass around me; all were seemingly asleep although none were sleeping. Of the white-clad lady to my left, I knew that she lay with her face propped in her hands and a novel open before her, but not once did I hear her turn its pages. And nobody said a word. We were all compelled to absolute inactivity, and had a lingering sense that little by little the heat was stifling all will and all energy. We might lie this way for years, for who could be bothered to so much as twitch a foot or lift a head or turn the pages of a novel? Even thought, which never rests, was dulled, for who could be bothered to think? And there was no longer any need to listen for the whisper out at sea; even our ears were shut now and then. The sound slipped by, we heard sporadically: a bumblebee buzzing, perhaps, a gate slamming closed. I knew that a parrot hung in a cage in the middle of the sunny wall of the hotel. No doubt it felt its feathers grow warm, yearned to shift its bony old carcass; I could hear it grab the metal bars with its beak and swing. But then a gate slammed shut again, so hard this time that the hinges jangled. Shortly afterwards, I heard a voice close by me saying: 'Do you see that?'

What was there to see, for who could be bothered to lift their head? Then came the sound of footsteps from the road down below, hasty footsteps; it must be a man and a woman running. I could hear the tramp of the man's boots and the slap of the lady's skirts. I stood up, my eyes blinded by the immensity of the sun, which sparkled and shattered in the air.

'Look there,' said the white-clad lady by my side. She pointed, and through the blinding white apple trees I now saw what was going on in the road.

Three people were running. First came a quick little barefoot lad. After him, a man no longer young, a local, dressed in blue shirtsleeves with a threadbare little yellow straw hat in one hand. Last came the lady, one of the summer guests. But she was trailing far behind, hindered by her white dress. She tried to gather it up, but failed, and so she ran onwards, her frock flapping like a white flag.

'Perhaps there's an angry bull,' said the lady by my side.

But that couldn't possibly be the explanation, because then the people would have no need to run as the gate was shut fast behind them.

By now all we sluggish summer folk had roused ourselves; some stood up and raised a hand to shade their eyes.

The runners were heading in our direction. A low fence separated the hotel grounds from the road. There was a small opening in this fence, with a wooden bar you merely had to push aside to pass through. The lad and the man reached it at almost the same time, but now the most comical thing happened: they were both in such a hurry that they got into a terrible muddle over this simple bar, fumbling at it and clearly quite confused as to whether they should jump over it, break it to pieces, crawl under it, or push it aside. And the sole result of all this fuss was that the lady in the white dress caught up with them. The lad proved the brightest of the three: he hopped over the fence a little further down, fell to his knees, got up again and hurried towards us. Once the man was left to his own devices, he quickly managed to shove the bar aside. The three people reached us at almost the same time, and we could tell at once from their gestures that something strange had happened. But they were all too upset to be able to tell their tale straight away. The man, the local, sputtered unintelligibly, his eyes bulging with fear, unable to find the words; the lady, quite out of breath, pressed her hand to her breast. But the lad was also quickest of speech.

The lad was the first to tell the tale.

It was still so early in the summer that only six or seven holiday guests had arrived. Of these, three were ladies, who worked at a large company in Kristiania, where staff holidays were portioned out among the employees from mid-May until late September. The summer season proper had not yet begun, but the ladies had to content themselves with taking their holiday whenever their turn should come. And then there were four of us gentlemen: an old bank clerk, a young student, a forestry inspector and the writer of these lines.

So far we had been more than a little unlucky with the weather: blustery by day, chilly by night and overcast. But then one day the summer flared up abruptly, heavy with heat and glowing with sun. And that is why the joy was so general, the idle wellbeing so pleasant on that morning we were disturbed by three people running along the road.

The little place where we now found ourselves was, incidentally, an exceedingly popular destination for summer guests, especially in July and August. A few short minutes' walk through a young spruce forest and before us lay the sea; far out there in the dark nights burned the beams of the lighthouse, flickering like northern lights across the sky. It was a fairly low landscape, an immense and somewhat rugged island. Very little of the land was cultivated, at least in the vicinity of the hotel, but a great plain stretched dozens of miles into its interior, a plain filled with heaps of rocks deposited by the moraine; here and there small tarns twinkled and riverbeds ran, and between them were marshy expanses overgrown with bushes and brushwood. Far out on this plain lay Gjærnæs Farm, on a carpet of green, well-tended fields and lush gardens. By day, a glimpse of it was visible from the gable room of the summer hotel, and by night, from the same vantage point, lights could be seen twinkling in the windows of the farm. When I arrived at the hotel, I expressly requested the gable room so that I could enjoy the magnificent view across the plain at my pleasure. I knew the people on the farm from previous visits: a brother and sister called Carsten and Hilde Gjærnæs.

Across the plain ran an old road that led with many twists and turns past the heaped rocks, around the tarns, over the brooks, and through the undergrowth and brushwood. A much-favoured route for a stroll, it took you from the summer hotel to the farm in half an hour or so. Once there, an opportunity might arise to greet Hilde, who was young and beautiful, or strike up a conversation with Carsten Gjærnæs – and in both cases, the excursion could be reckoned a success.

On the evening before the events I shall now recount, I had taken a walk across the plain.

I left the hotel just after half past nine, once the evening meal was over. I was alone and walked with some haste, for the evening air felt chill and clammy. A little after ten o'clock, I found myself close to the farm and thought there might be some sport in a conversation, a hand of cards or a game of chess with Carsten Gjærnæs. It was precisely the time at which he was in the habit of settling down in his study to while away the hours until midnight. I took it for granted that I would be welcome, since Carsten Gjærnæs was a man inclined to be sociable, and I knew him fairly well.

But I must confess I had another little hidden motive: what if Hilde had not yet retired for the night – might I perhaps have a chance to exchange a few words with her? She was, as I have said, a very pretty girl and here in this wilderness I was feeling the lack of a woman's company. I found the three highly strung business ladies at the hotel quite unbearable with their constant prattle about whether they were growing fat or turning brown, or whether I would like to accompany them to some spot where they could pick water lilies.

I went through the garden gate and into the farmyard where the black dog Hektor lay in his kennel; he growled and then, when I feigned not to notice, waddled out slowly, dragging his chain behind him. He kept on howling and growling, which caused me some puzzlement, for Hektor had always struck me as a placid dog.

As I was about to go through the front door, the farm steward came up and barred my way.

'Pardon me,' he said. 'The squire cannot be disturbed right now.'

I stood staring at the man.

'What is the matter?' I asked. 'Are you ill?'

The man was pale; I could see it despite the dim light. He stood there in the passageway, leaning against the doorframe. That could signify he was so weak he was close to collapse, but it could also mean that he would not let me past at any price and intended, by blocking the doorway, to show that I should not come by him.

'I am not ill,' he said.

'Is your master ill, then?'

14

'No.'

'Does he have visitors?'

'No, he has absolutely no visitors. He is alone with his sister.'

I did not entirely understand why I was being denied entry so I continued with my questions.

'Can it be that I have caused him some offence?' I murmured.

'Not at all,' answered the steward. 'But Mr Gjærnæs cannot receive you this evening.'

I looked at the man more closely again, by now quite convinced that he was indeed unusually pale. I remember thinking then: why doesn't he ask if he can send his master my greetings, or whether I have come on some errand. I asked again: 'How did you happen to be out here in the passageway, ready to meet me?'

'The mistress saw you coming.'

'Miss Hilde?'

'Yes. And she asked me not to let you in. I'm here on orders.'

I turned abruptly and walked away. I did not take my leave of the man, did not so much as nod at him. I walked straight across the farmyard. The dog growled louder than before. There was a short cut through the garden, a path I knew well. I had walked along it many times before and I walked along it now. But then I did something that shows I had begun to nurse a suspicion that some peculiar business was afoot. I stopped in the darkness of the garden, beneath the cover of the trees, and stood there listening and looking over at the house.

I could tell that the master had no guests, as the only lights burning were in the study and the room beside it. The light in his study was extinguished and then lit again a couple of times. Just once, light winked in all the windows facing the farmyard when some person walked through the rooms with a lamp. It must have been Carsten Gjærnæs, as his own room lay in darkness while this was happening. It was remarkable how much activity there was at the big farm. I listened tensely, and at one point it seemed to me that I heard unusually loud or excitable voices from within.

As I stood there thinking that I should go, I saw one of the small side doors in the main building open. I knew this side door led into the mistress's apartment, into Miss Hilde's three small private rooms.

Out of the door came a man in a green hunting jacket. He had a rifle under his arm, its barrel pointing downwards. He stood on the upper step and a woman came out too. It was Hilde. She held out a hand to him, smiled and said a few words. Then he left, turned around to wave a hand and she waved back. From my vantage point, I could see it all quite clearly. I knew the man in the hunting jacket well, a pleasant young chap who was staying with the rest of us at the hotel. He was a forestry inspector called Blinde.

I found myself greatly interested, without being quite certain of the reason why. I stole around the back of a thick tree trunk because I did not want him to catch sight of me as I spied on him. Now Hilde had gone inside. She had plainly made no secret of escorting this man out. She had spoken so loudly to him that even I, standing towards the end of the garden, could hear her voice, although I was unable to distinguish the words; and she slammed the door, then turned the key with a click.

A mere ten paces away from me the man stood and lit his pipe. His face glowed in the light of the match. He had a reddish-brown beard, and firm, chiselled features. He threw the matchstick to the ground and trod it out. Then he turned his face into the wind as if to scent the air, a habit born of life in field and forest: he wanted to see what the weather was doing. Before going on, he tugged his hat further down over his eyes, then he left. He took the path across the desolate plain towards the summer hotel. I waited a few minutes, for I did not want him to know that I had been spying, and then I followed.

By the time I came out onto the plain, he had vanished beyond the nearest patch of marshland. I could no longer hear his footsteps and no noise came from the farm; the wind had blown by and all was silent around me. It is odd to be out on such a plain on a summer's night: it becomes so endless, as the horizon disappears and the plain creeps up to meet the heavens – you cannot tell where the sky begins and the plain ends. In the blind half-light, the heaped boulders and rocky outcrops and, here or there, the occasional tree, assume strange and mysterious shapes. As I came over a stretch where the plain sloped down steadily to the sea, I felt a chill breath from the ocean and turned up the collar of my jacket. I looked out, I could see the ocean. The sea is always cool at night; I could hear the long swells rolling stealthily in and breaking on the shore. Ripples of shifting sand were blown along, and from these shifting sands protruded wretched, wind-blasted coastal pines, their canopies flattened and twisted inland like broken fans.

I knew that this area was unsafe, that the occasional tinker sloop often came sneaking through the skerries by night. Belly full to bursting, sails filthy and ragged, with superfluous poles trailing in the water behind it and oars bristling, the sloop would settle on the rock like an insect. And then the tinkers would go ashore and raise hell among the lone souls that lived or wandered there. But I was not afraid, I simply remembered all this as I walked across the open expanse; I had a stout cane in my hand, an ivory-headed walking stick. I walked quickly onwards across the plain and buried myself in the shadows.

Close by the summer hotel the road ran through a little spruce forest. It was fairly dark here. I stopped in the middle

17

of the wood as a peculiar sound reached my ears. What could it be? The noise came from a long way off and I caught it only intermittently. It sounded almost like the rattling of metal links, a thrumming of chains some ten miles distant. I carried on walking; I walked for five minutes and suddenly caught sight of something moving in the darkness a few feet away. Seeing at once that it must be a person, I tightened my grip on my cane and walked out in a wide arc.

A man was standing there, a short man with a broad-brimmed hat on his head. I realised that if I walked any further, I'd have the man behind me, so I stopped at once. And as I stood there, motionless, the man came slowly towards me. Now that I recognised him, I began to feel ridiculous and regretted having taken a detour; I tucked my cane nonchalantly beneath my arm. At the same time, though, I couldn't help feeling pleased that the man was not somebody else, a stranger. He belonged to the place, after all; I couldn't immediately remember his name, but he was a mild-mannered fisherman I'd spoken to often in the past. I said, 'Out so late?'

Instead of answering this profundity, the man cocked an ear to the sky and asked, 'Do you hear that?'

'What?'

'Hush,' said the man, listening.

And now the sound came again, that infinitely distant sound of loose chains rattling.

'What is it?' I asked.

'The iron chariot,' the man replied, gravely. 'It's a long time since I last heard it.'

The iron chariot. It occurred to me that I'd once heard about this. An odd tale to which I had paid little heed. I no longer remembered what it was, but the night and the darkness filled me with a sense that there was something eerie about it.

Abruptly, I seized the man by the arm and walked alongside him.

'The iron chariot?' I asked. 'How long is it since you heard it?'

'Four years – it was the night old man Gjærnæs died.'

'Who owns the chariot?'

'Yes, indeed, who does own the chariot?' the man replied and shook his head.

I did not question him further, for now we emerged from the forest, and the red-striped awning at the front of the hotel drove away all the atmosphere of the plain. And we could no longer hear the iron chariot either, since the forest lay between us and the plain, shutting out any sound.

I went up to my gable room and opened both windows. The first thing I saw was a dim light twinkling far, far away. So the people at Gjærnæs Farm had not yet retired for the night. Suddenly, I was interested in knowing when that light would be put out. I stationed myself by the window, but when I became tired of waiting I paced back and forth across the floor, smoked a few cigarettes, then returned to the window, thinking: now the light must be out – but still it was twinkling over there. A whole hour passed. Then all at once I felt the night grow warm and muggy, and when I put a hand out of the window, a couple of heavy raindrops fell upon it. The air stood still, then the warm rain descended upon us and the heat was pressed towards the earth. I listened and watched. And now I heard it again, this distant rattling of iron, but the sound was even further off than before; for long stretches I couldn't hear it any longer, then came a single, faint sound, followed again by silence, and then I heard the rattling for a minute or more.

The iron chariot. I closed the windows; the sky outside was lightening; somewhere, day must have crept over the mountains. I saw the trees become slick with damp. A last glance across the plain, where the light burned still. I rolled down the blind.

The true, languorous, stifling heat of summer had arrived. It was the next morning that we five summer folk lay out on the grass, bathing in the sun and heat.

It was then that the three people came running: the lad, the fisherman and the lady in the white dress.

They had something strange to tell us, but the lad was quickest of speech. He was the first to tell the tale. He said:

'We've found a murdered man up on the road.'

II

The Dead Man

'WE'VE FOUND A MURDERED MAN up on the road,' said the lad. His eyes were like two fever spots in his face, and his entire body trembled.

'I saw him too,' stammered the old fisherman.

'But I saw him first,' said the lad.

Beyond this, little more was said for some seconds. The shocking announcement struck us with a kind of paralysis; I could see how incredible this occurrence appeared to the people around me, how absurd it seemed, how perturbing – precisely because it presented such an abrupt and violent contrast to our present comfortable state of warm summer calm: the wind wafted gently over the meadows, myriad birdsong filled the air and from the sea below came the noisy, rapid pulse of a motor boat. A glass door was jerked open up in the summer hotel and I heard the landlady complaining about the maids. Suddenly the bank clerk cried: 'But good heavens, we must go up there!'

We menfolk set off at once, half-walking half-running and staring straight ahead. The ladies demurred briefly, then followed us at a slight distance. And the lad ran like an eager little puppy, sometimes ahead of us and sometimes getting under our feet. He led the way.

We came through the forest, which took no more than five minutes, and there we met some people whom we swept along with us. We came out onto the desolate plain, which lay burning desert-like beneath the steaming sun. We stayed on the path that ran along the edge of the forest. As we ran we spoke to the lad.

'Are you sure,' we asked, 'that you saw it right?'

'Yes, it's quite true,' replied the lad. 'I was meant to drive the cattle out onto the plain, but then I found him.'

'How did you find him? Did you stumble over him?'

'No, but the big bull was standing sniffing at the grass with his muzzle. I yelled at him but he wouldn't leave the spot, so I went over to see what the matter was. And then I saw the man down in a hollow. He was lying on his front with his face to the ground.'

'And then what?'

'I was scared stiff and ran off as fast as I could. Down in the woods I met a man carrying a tin pail. After I told him what I'd seen, we both ran back to the place, and then he said at once…'

'Yes, so then I said,' interrupted the man himself, who was running alongside the lad. 'So I said straight away that he'd been killed.'

'How could you tell?'

'His head,' muttered the man. 'His head was hideous. But we're nearly there now.'

And with that, we arrived.

Down in a little hollow, so close to the edge of the forest that

22

he was touched by its shadows, lay the man. The student, who was soon to take his medical examinations, was the first to reach him and I heard him cry, 'It is Forestry Inspector Blinde.'

And now we all recognised him, as did the ladies who arrived soon afterwards, somewhat short of breath. The dead man was the forestry inspector I had seen leaving Miss Hilde's apartment the night before. He was still dressed in the same green hunting jacket and had his rifle with him.

We could all see at once that he must have been killed, for there was a gaping wound in the back of his head. The poor fellow had been hurled headlong by the blow and he must have died instantly, for his face was buried in the soft soil. He had fallen on top of the barrel of his rifle so only the stock was protruding.

The student asked for a pocket-handkerchief. Having obtained one from one of the ladies he laid it carefully over the wound. Then he got up and said: 'Nobody must move him.'

One of the ladies sobbed. The scene had a peculiar atmosphere to it, reminiscent of a quiet burial at a simple country church on a fine spring day. The air was so marvellously bright and translucent, the chalk-white kerchief over the murdered man's head stirred slightly, trembled at the edges. Out on the plain, the sun shone golden upon the cattle, and the beasts gazed at us with their great, stupid eyes.

I am certain that nobody there at that moment was thinking about how the murder might have come to pass, nor did it occur to anybody to consider who the murderer might be. Everybody was too thoroughly absorbed in the matter at hand, in what had already happened; there was no room for other thoughts: impressions had not yet become fixed and the image of the event, of the fact at hand, was not yet fully formed. Only once the incredible had been confirmed as fact in people's minds

23

would the question arise: But how did this come about?

The little medical student was clearly a born detective. He leapt up when he heard the little lad say, 'Here's the hat.'

And when the lad bent down to pick it up, the student dashed over at once and seized him by the arm.

'Leave the hat where it is!' he bellowed.

And the hat was left where it was.

It was a green felt hat of the kind that hunters wear. It had a large button on the left-hand side and a smart band around the crown; it belonged to the dead forestry inspector.

The medical student explained, with an expert air, 'A crime has taken place here,' he said. 'Our mutual friend, Forestry Inspector Blinde, has been killed by a person unknown. As far as I can tell his death must have been almost instantaneous, and was caused by a blow to the back of the head with a blunt instrument.'

This expression, 'a blunt instrument', with its veritable whiff of jail and police, made the ladies shudder; they gradually edged further and further away from the dreadful spot until, presently, only we menfolk were left standing around the body. The medical student was eager as ever.

'His hat is over there,' he continued. 'Naturally, it fell off when he was struck. It would be best to leave it untouched until the detective arrives.'

'The detective?' I asked. 'Are you expecting a detective?'

'Yes, of course,' replied the medical student. 'We must wire for a detective; I know of an excellent man in Kristiania.'

'But it will take him a great many hours to get here,' I objected. 'And we can't just leave the dead man lying here.'

This prospect gave the medical student pause for thought.

'We cannot let him lie out here overnight,' he said. 'If the detective cannot be here by midnight, then we must have the dead man carried indoors.'

Since I travel a great deal, I always have about me a list of the railway and steamship routes. I took out my tables and sat down in the grass to study them. The medical student knelt down at my side and eagerly craned his neck over my tables.

'It is twelve o'clock now,' I said. 'Are you quite certain the policeman you want to get hold of is in Kristiania?'

'Pretty certain. I have his address.'

'Very well. Then we shall send him a telegram. This telegram can hardly be in his possession before two o'clock, which means he cannot catch the fast train that leaves Kristiania in half an hour. He must wait for the ordinary passenger train at 5.13.'

'He is quite capable of ordering an extra train to be laid on.'

'He will hardly do that; it is not a question of preventing a crime, after all, but of solving a mystery that has already come to light. We must assume that he will wait until 5.13. He won't be able to get away especially quickly, either. The journey from Kristiania to our nearest town takes five hours by rail. So he cannot possibly arrive in time to catch the afternoon boat out here.'

'He will most certainly find a fast motorboat.'

'That may be so, but even a very fast motorboat cannot make the journey in under four hours. He cannot be here before two in the morning.'

The medical student shook his head.

'Ah, but you don't know the detective I'm talking about,' he said.

'Nonetheless,' I replied. 'We must consider the circumstances before us. Since it seems most likely that the policeman cannot be here before two o'clock tomorrow morning, I believe we must arrange to have the dead man brought indoors.'

'Yes, yes,' replied the medical student. 'There is certainly nothing else for it. But shall we take him down with us to the summer hotel?'

I was about to reply when I was interrupted by a man pushing his way through the crowd of people around us.

It was the local police chief.

News of the sinister discovery had spread rapidly. Somebody had telephoned the police chief from the summer hotel and he had cycled over in a matter of minutes.

He was sorely confused by the whole unaccustomed business; I could see it in his pale face and trembling hands. He also recognised the man in the green hunting jacket straight away, and muttered, 'Poor chap! What in the world is this about?'

'He has been killed,' answered the medical student. 'You can see that for yourself.'

The police chief bent over the body and whispered, 'Yes indeed, yes indeed.'

'We have agreed that the dead man must be taken inside,' continued the medical student. 'The detective can hardly be here before early tomorrow morning.'

The medical student explained to him that a police expert from the capital was best placed to deal with this case and the police chief agreed. He thanked the medical student courteously when he took it upon himself to summon the detective from Kristiania to the scene of the murder. The police chief appeared all too happy to be relieved of a degree of responsibility.

But where should the dead man be taken?

Once again, there was talk of the summer hotel, and the police chief thought the dead man should, of course, be taken there, to the place where he had been staying when still alive. I objected that this would be tantamount to driving away most of the guests – all of the ladies at least. Another place must be found.

26

And then the police chief remembered that there was an uninhabited cabin some minutes' walk away, a little sand-digger's hut. It was decided at once that the dead man should be taken there.

There was plenty of assistance at hand. A makeshift stretcher was rigged up. The dead man was lifted onto it and his rifle placed by his side.

The dead man's face had not been injured at all. It was only slightly soiled with earth and sand.

The medical student seized my arm.

'Why, look at him,' he said.

'What is it?'

'Look at his face. It's smiling.'

'It seems quite expressionless to me,' I replied.

The medical student took a long look at the dead man.

'He was smiling,' he muttered. 'A disdainful smile crossed his face just before he was dealt the fatal blow.'

The medical student suggested covering the dead man's face with his hunting hat. It was done. Four of those present then bore the dead man to the sand-digger's hut, whose dark grey walls were just visible against the brown heathland. The police chief walked beside them. I held back a little, for I have always had an insurmountable aversion to bodies and burials.

But where was the medical student?

I turned back. Believe it or not, there he was on all fours at the murder scene, sniffing around in the soil like a dog.

I had to smile. He was a young chap, hardly more than nineteen or twenty years old. He had probably been stuffed full of gripping yarns and fancied playing detective. He was searching for tracks – as if that were the way crimes were solved these days!

Cupping my hand into a makeshift megaphone I called out

his name.

'Hey, you!' My voice cut across the plain. 'Aren't we going to go with them?'

He got up slowly, brushing the dirt from his knees and sauntered towards me.

'A strange business,' he said. 'It cannot be long since he was killed.'

So now the time for reflection had come. The observations had been gathered and nothing more was happening. We were beginning to think back, and the first question was: when did this happen? The next would inevitably be: how did it happen?

I answered, 'Let's ask the people at the hotel when he went out. I didn't see him at breakfast.'

We reached the ladies, who were standing in a huddle terrifying each other. We enquired, and nobody had seen the forestry inspector – but he had been in the habit of getting up early, much earlier than the other guests.

Half an hour later, we were all gathered on the hotel veranda. The medical student had been driven to the telegraph office. We were all awaiting his return, keeping watch for him down the road. The police chief cycled by in a great hurry. The odd person went running past. Everybody now knew what had happened and a sinister atmosphere had settled upon the farms; we saw people stop work in the fields, some dashed into their houses with their tools on their backs. A gate clanged – it was the medical student running back from the telegraph office. He swung his cap so that the red silk lining gleamed in the sun and, while still a long way off, he called out to us: 'I spoke to him on the telephone.'

He was thoroughly worked up and terribly eager.

'I have spoken to the man himself on the telephone,' he repeated, as he stepped noisily up onto the veranda.

He did not mention the policeman's name, but we all knew who he meant.

'Is he coming?' we all cried at once.

'Yes, he's coming as quickly as possible, but he couldn't say exactly when.'

'Let us not lose sight of the facts of the matter,' I slipped in. 'Who knows whether this was a murder?'

'What's that?'

'Perhaps it was an accident.'

'Impossible, unthinkable,' said some. And we debated the matter at length. Suddenly one of the ladies asked, 'But who in the world can have killed him?'

Yes, who? That was the mystery. The forestry inspector certainly had no enemies that we knew of. He was a very peaceable chap, exceedingly reserved. He preferred not to mingle with the other guests, seldom spoke at mealtimes and took long, solitary walks.

'You knew him from before, didn't you?' the medical student said to me. 'Perhaps you can think of something…'

'I only knew him in passing,' I answered. 'I have met him perhaps two or three times altogether. I have no explanations to offer.'

Could it have been a case of murder with intent to rob?

Most certainly not: the medical student and I had both noticed that Blinde was still in possession of both his diamond ring and his gold watch chain.

Now the landlady arrived and informed us that the forestry inspector's bed had not been slept in. He had definitely not come home the night before.

So it was possible that the murder could have happened the previous evening.

The medical student was somewhat dismayed.

'I might have been able to see that from the tracks,' he muttered. 'It rained last night after all. When did it start raining?'

Most thought the rain had started at around midnight.

The medical student looked at me. 'Something seems to have occurred to you,' he said.

'Yes,' I answered. 'The rain started at almost exactly one o'clock.'

'How do you know?'

'I was up. I felt the first heavy drops fall. And I can tell you, ladies and gentlemen, that I walked across the plain between eleven o'clock and half past the hour.'

'Did you hear anything?'

'I heard a carriage rattling along a road a long way off; that was all.'

'Had you come from the farm?'

'Yes, from Gjærnæs Farm… Who was the last person to see him alive?' I asked suddenly.

The answers were various.

Some had seen him last at the supper table. The landlady had seen him go up to his room an hour after that. One of the ladies had seen him in his hunting jacket with his rifle slung over his shoulder at half-past nine. He had been on his way out then, had greeted the lady amicably and said a few words to the effect that there would soon be rain. He had pointed up at the sky and said: 'See those fluffy little clouds scudding across the sky there, Miss? The rain shower is driving them before it.'

'But what about you?' asked the medical student. 'Perhaps you saw him even later?'

'Half-past ten,' I answered. 'That was the last time I saw

30

Forestry Inspector Blinde alive.'

I now told them what had happened to me on the previous evening: how I had seen Blinde leave Gjærnæs Farm and vanish over the plain. I presented my whole account very carefully, saying nothing of the fact that the murdered man had come out of Miss Hilde's rooms. When I had finished, my listeners sat there for a long time, silent and deep in thought. The ladies looked diffidently at one another and the medical student remarked, 'It was a bit odd that you weren't allowed into the farm, wasn't it? Young Gjærnæs is usually such a sociable man.'

'My impression,' I replied, 'is that something unusual was going on at the farm. The steward looked quite upset and his tone of voice when he refused me entry to the house was oddly urgent. One way or another, I believe I was as unwelcome as could be at that precise moment, and I am sure that it had nothing to do with my person.'

'Do you mean that something was going on at the farm?'

'Yes, I do.'

'But you saw nothing unusual?'

'No, and I heard nothing either. But the lights that flickered from room to room suggested there was a certain amount of movement going on inside.'

The medical student murmured that perhaps the forestry inspector's death might be connected with the peculiar excitement that appeared to have been afoot at the usually peaceful farm.

'How did Blinde look yesterday evening? Was he agitated?'

'Not in the least,' I replied. 'He was as placid as ever; his face didn't betray the slightest agitation. He lit his pipe when he stopped about ten paces away from where I was standing, right beside the big pear tree, and the match lit up his face so that I could see every feature. No, he was very calm...'

And so the talk buzzed on throughout the afternoon. The mysterious crime was still so perplexing that the same questions constantly came up time and time again; imagination came into play, the small improbabilities began to swirl about, a terrible nervousness came over the ladies, who could barely eat – they picked away at the lightest dishes and left their glasses of milk half-drunk, so intent were they on making each other jump with shuddersome talk of the murder. What was the forestry inspector doing there at Gjærnæs Farm so late at night? It started with a mysterious glint in a pair of female eyes, a tight-lipped smile that betrayed some special knowledge – and before long the romance was in full flow. The forestry inspector and Miss Hilde had been seen together several times. Lord knows what business Blinde had down here in this part of the country if it wasn't to meet Miss Hilde, with all those great forests of his own to wander round in. Out of consideration, I had not mentioned Hilde's name: I was well aware of the ladies' powers of deduction in a certain direction, and that is why I hadn't told them I'd seen Blinde leave Hilde's private apartment at half-past ten at night. But still the ladies scrabbled after any unlikely detail suggestive of a romantic drama; they half won over the medical student and when, late in the afternoon, the rumour spread that Miss Hilde was driving past along the road, hordes of ladies and gentleman stormed the veranda, tumbling over one other in their sheer eagerness to catch a glimpse of their heroine.

Miss Hilde was driving along in a four-wheeler. She was alone in the buggy and drove swiftly, reins gripped tightly and gaze fixed unswervingly ahead. On her head was a white flannel cap secured in her thick brown hair with a long pin – I could see the pin clearly, see its gilt head gleaming. And I could see her profile clearly too: she was paler than usual and there was a tightness about her features, as though she were on the point of tears. She dashed by in a terrible hurry, took a right turn and the buggy vanished in a cloud of dust.

'To the police chief,' somebody said. 'She's off to see the police chief, he lives over that way.'

Barely five minutes later, she drove back again in the opposite direction. But now the police chief was in the buggy with her. She had her whip at the ready and her horse was streaming with sweat.

The ladies were of the view that she wanted to see the dead man, because nobody was allowed into the sand-digger's hut unless the police chief himself was present. And so she had fetched him. She had returned so quickly that she must have hauled the police chief out of his office as if it were a matter of life and death. And how she urged that horse! Long after the buggy had vanished into the depths of the forest, we could hear the scrape of its wheels against the road.

As I heard the sound of the buggy being gradually muffled by the forest before finally dying away, a small event from the previous night came to mind: my meeting with the fisherman. I remembered that he, too, had come from the plain; that he, like me, had stood listening to the distant sound of rolling carriage wheels. But what was it he had spoken of? The iron chariot...

I saw him in my mind's eye, standing there in the darkness, small and scrawny, and shaking his head at my question: 'Who owns the iron chariot? Yes, indeed, who does own it?'

Over the course of the afternoon, some of the locals came to the hotel. They wanted to hear more about the sinister events. They spoke in circumspections, voices low as those of funeral guests, pumping the serving staff and the landlady for information; some were bold enough to approach the guests, striking up conversations with great, vague observations about the crops and the weather. All had been up to the sand-digger's hut and the scene of the murder. The storekeeper told us that Miss Hilde had been into the hut and had seen the body, but had driven swiftly away again. She had not wept, but had been so terribly pale – deathly pale with taut features. It was curious that none of the locals ventured any definite statements about the cause of the crime or the possible identity of the murderer, although their idle chat and the expressions on their faces suggested that they had their own views on the matter. They spoke about the plain. There is something peculiar about that plain. Many things have happened out on that plain. And the old farm appeared to have its share of secrets, too, secrets people knew about but preferred not to discuss.

The evening descended, still and beautiful. We sat out on the veranda and the conversation about the inevitable topic went back and forth, back and forth, the ladies becoming ever more tremulous as the daylight faded to grey. We still had that sense of incredulity, of impossibility, because the contrast was so stark: out there on the plain brooded dark horror, yet here we were, we few summer guests, sitting together in this mild and peaceful evening. We listened for the slap of oars from the sea and footsteps from the roads, surrounded by the delicate chirp of birdsong, as the cigar smoke rose straight into the air, a wonderful shade of pale blue. When the mosquitoes became too irksome we moved into the lounge. Although the ladies were sleepy, they preferred not to retire for the night because they were too scared of being alone.

Suddenly I heard somebody call my name; the cry came from out on the veranda – a voice I didn't recall having heard before.

'Somebody is calling you,' said the medical student.

'Yes, I heard it myself.'

I got up swiftly, walked over and opened both of the veranda doors. There was not a living soul to be seen out on the veranda. Just empty basket chairs and a table. And on the table stood a couple of bottles of soda water and a few empty glasses. For a moment, I was quite nonplussed, but then I heard my name being called again and now I saw a yellow straw hat beneath the veranda. When I walked forward a few paces, the straw hat vanished and a head of grey hair came into view amid the foliage. The man standing there calling me was the fisherman from the previous night.

I leant out over the balustrade and said, in an inexplicable effusion of benevolence, 'Oh, it's you. What a pleasure to see you again. We spoke yesterday evening, did we not?'

'I've been at work all day,' replied the man. 'Otherwise I'd've come long ago.'

'What may I do for you?'

The man squinted up at me with his clouded white eyes.

'Well, isn't it peculiar what happened?' he said.

'The murder, you mean?'

'Yes. I've heard he was killed yesterday night.'

'That seems to be the case.'

'At around eleven?'

'It can't be said for certain. The last time he was seen alive was half-past ten. I saw him myself.'

'Well, isn't that strange, isn't that strange...' muttered the man. 'You heard it too, didn't you?' he added enquiringly.

'What?'

'The iron chariot. Both of us stood and listened to it, didn't we? The iron chariot rolling along, far off in the distance.'

A peculiar sensation began to quiver in my chest.

'Had you come from the plain?' I asked the man.

'Yes,' he replied. 'I walked past the sand-digger's hut at half-past ten.'

'Did you hear anything?'

'I heard nothing but the iron chariot.'

'No cries?'

'No.'

'Wait,' I said. 'I shall be back directly.'

I fetched my hat and my indispensable ivory-headed cane.

I walked out onto the road and beckoned the man over.

'Come with me,' I said. 'Tell me what you know about the iron chariot. Isn't it some old legend?'

'An old legend,' muttered the man uncomprehendingly. He shook his head again. 'Let's sit ourselves down somewhere,' he added. 'It's so hard to talk while we're walking. Besides, you walk so fast and I'm tired. I've been at work all day.'

He pointed to a rock that stood in the nearest patch of pastureland like a shining skull in the lush grass. We walked over the meadow, damp with evening dew.

'It's getting late,' I said, as we sat down. I was familiar with the slow ways of the local people and was keen for the man to hurry up.

'Yes,' said the man. 'At just this time yesterday, it had already happened.'

'Where did you first hear the iron chariot?'

'When I was already in the woods. I know the sound well, there's no mistaking it. I've heard the iron chariot before, I can tell you.'

'When?'

'Four years ago. The same night old man Gjærnæs passed away.'

'Was he murdered too?'

'No, he drowned. His hat and cane were found washed ashore down on the big sandy beach, and a few days later we found his rowing boat, capsized and knocking against the rocks.'

'But the body?'

'It was never found.'

'How old was the man?'

'Over fifty. Nobody could understand why on earth the old man had decided to row out to sea in a little open boat.'

'What a strange notion.'

'Yes, very strange. We talked a bit about that, us folk here in the area. Just among ourselves, like. We had our suspicions.'

'Suicide?'

The man evaded my question.

'Everybody must answer for his own actions,' he said.

'But you heard the iron chariot that night, then?'

'Yes, I heard it just as clearly as last night. It's an old farm, the Gjærnæs' place, and it has a few strange secrets, I can tell you.'

The man now launched into a long tale about the sinister portents that were often to be seen at the old farm. According to one legend, the man who had owned the farm a hundred years ago or more had driven to his death in an iron chariot. He was a reserved, eccentric type who had travelled a great deal around the world, and about whom nobody had a good word to say. He had squandered his inheritance on countless half-crazed inventions. He had a particular obsession with horses and peculiar vehicles. In the end, he had a chariot manufactured that was made entirely of iron. With its two wheels and the large protective guard at the front it was not unlike the war chariots of old used by the ancient Hebrews, the kind you might see in an illustrated Bible. It was in this chariot that he drove to his death one night, out upon the plain. Since then, whenever some terrible thing was about to happen at Gjærnæs Farm, or whenever somebody was about to die, people always heard the iron chariot rattling its way across the plain. But nobody had seen it and it never left any tracks upon the road. Some claimed the iron chariot still lay hidden somewhere on the farm, concealed in some securely locked room in the huge barn building. The last time the chariot had been heard was four years ago, the night old Gjærnæs had died. Many rumours had spread about this man: his financial affairs were said to be in some disorder and it was plain to all that the farm had fallen into disrepair. But still, his vigorous, energetic son had managed to keep the whole thing above water, and even to pay off some of his father's debts… All this, the fisherman told me in a halting, cautious manner, as if fearful of my distrust.

'Now, we are the only ones who heard the iron chariot last night,' he said at length. 'And I wanted to ask you if I should tell other people what I heard.'

'Why not?'

The fisherman sat silent for a long time.

In the end, he muttered, 'They don't believe me. I've been to the parson and told him about all the strange things I've seen on land and sea both. I've been to the schoolmaster too. But they just smiled at me and said I had a lively imagination. Now, though, I think to myself: maybe you'll get a fair hearing, with a man from the capital, a man of letters, on your side. Yes, indeed, because after all you heard the iron chariot too, didn't you?'

Once again, I was surprised by the fisherman's eagerness. I assured him that I would gladly stand by him.

'I did indeed hear some carriage rolling across the plain last night,' I said. 'But I cannot vouch for the fact that it was a phantom chariot, of course.'

'It can't have been any other carriage,' replied the fisherman decisively. 'Look at the roads. It rained last night, didn't it, and any carriage as heavy as the one we heard must have left tracks behind it; but you try looking – you'll soon see there aren't any wheel tracks on the roads. In this neck of the woods, the only people with horses are Gjærnæs and the parson.'

I had no wish to go into the matter further, so I told him he could tell his tale to a man who would be coming the next day.

'What's your name?' I asked.

'Jan Jansen,' he replied.

'Very well, Jan Jansen. Early tomorrow, a policeman will arrive from Kristiania on the mail boat; speak to him. He will certainly listen to you with interest.'

I lit a cigar to ward off the mosquitoes. The fisherman sat in silence for a long time, staring ahead despondently.

'There's a wind blowing up,' he said.

'Wind?' I exclaimed. 'But it is quite still here now. Look how the smoke from my cigar spreads out around us and lies in the air like blue veins.'

Pointing over the forest and out to sea, the fisherman answered: 'The southerly wind. When you hear that singing sound from the sea, far out there in the skerries, it means the wind's on its way.'

I listened. And then indeed it seemed to me that my ears were filled with a faint, incessant soughing, the kind of noise you do not hear unless you listen out for it, but that then becomes the only thing you can hear. Yet the night was still entirely windless, the light was merely drowsing, the colours had now faded and the trees stood etched against the sky like skeletons of ash.

Suddenly, the fisherman turned his head and leapt to his feet; he was listening, listening so intently that his mouth hung half-open.

'What do you hear?'

'I think I can hear...'

He listened again for a long time, but then sat down again calmly upon the rock and muttered: 'No, it was nothing.'

The fisherman was right. During the night, the wind picked

up. When I went up to my room at around half-past one, the windows were rattling on their hinges and the draught tore the door from my grasp, slamming it shut with a crash. I did not light my lamp but stood by my window a while, staring out across the plain towards Gjærnæs Farm: no lights were twinkling there now.

The wind was blowing straight towards me. It rose up from the ocean, bearing a wet gust of salt sea inland with it. It seized hold of the trees and rocked their mighty canopies, filled the woods with a great soughing so that the whole forest seemed to be sweeping towards me, and its great breath rolled through the yellow wheat fields in vast swells. As I pulled my flapping jacket about me, I felt an icy chill in my armpits. The warm blanket of heat that had lain over us all day was ripped to shreds at last and swept away by the wind.

I seized the window to close it but stopped suddenly when I caught a sound far off in the distance, a metallic rattling borne to me on the gusts of wind, and which rose and fell along with them. The sound was coming from the plain.

It was the iron chariot again.

III

The Old Farm

THE NEXT DAY, LATE IN THE MORNING, I woke with a start and sensed at once that I was not alone in my room. I raised myself up in bed and let my gaze wander round. A black box stood on my table, a box that did not belong to me, and that I had definitely never seen before. It was a camera. On a chair by the table sat a middle-aged man.

I sank back in my bed, still so dazed with sleep that I did not understand a thing.

A calm, amiable voice said, 'Lie there...just lie still; don't let me disturb you.'

It must be him, I thought, the policeman.

I asked, 'How did you get into my room?'

'Quite simply,' replied the amiable voice. 'Through the door.'

'You must have moved quietly. I am an exceptionally light sleeper.'

'Yes,' replied the man. 'I knew you were sleeping so I let

myself in very carefully. I didn't make any noise.'

Once again, I half sat up in bed, staring at the man in confusion, and asked, 'Why didn't you want to make any noise?'

'So as not to disturb you.'

The unknown gentleman smiled, a smile that expressed both goodwill and sarcasm. From where I lay in my bed, I was able to observe him very closely. I guessed his age at between thirty-five and forty. He was of average height and broad of shoulder. His head seemed somewhat too small for his thick, strong neck; he had thinning hair, a moustache threaded with grey and a black-framed pince-nez. He had peculiar eyes, which flitted about constantly. When he narrowed them, they lay behind the lenses of his pince-nez like two black slits, giving his face a sarcastic and sceptical expression; but when he looked at me sharply, his eyes became unnaturally large and very piercing. He did not seem entirely pleasant.

'Who are you?' I asked.

'I'm sure you have already guessed that,' he replied. 'My name is Asbjørn Krag.'

'The policeman?'

'Detective,' he corrected me. 'The term 'policeman' implies that one is employed in the service of the state. It is quite some time since I have worked for a wage. I am entirely my own master and therefore call myself a private investigator. You are, incidentally, quite right: you sleep extremely lightly.'

'I beg your pardon?'

'One brief glance was all it took to make you open your eyes.'

'Can you wake the sleeping with your gaze?'

'Good heavens, yes. It's very easy. Had I known you slept so lightly I would not have looked at you so intensely.'

'Why not?'

'I always find it interesting to watch sleeping people. And

listen to them too. Some people talk in their sleep, you know.'

'What do you want from me?'

'I want to talk to you about the murder. I am told you were the last person to see the murdered man alive.'

'Yes, I saw him at half-past ten that night.'

'And he was killed fairly close to eleven.'

My face must have reflected my astonishment at the man's blunt certainty, for he added, 'It is hardly difficult to conclude as much. It is a half-hour walk from the farm to the scene of the murder.'

'But we cannot know that he hadn't been elsewhere too,' I objected.

'You are forgetting the rain,' replied the detective. 'It is clear from the tracks that the unfortunate wretch fell before the rain started.'

I had no answer to that. Mr Asbjørn Krag stood up.

'I shall take a stroll outside while you get dressed,' he said. 'I rarely have the opportunity to spend any time in the countryside so it is only wise to make the most of the few hours at my disposal. What delightful air.'

'Will you be leaving so soon?'

'Possibly. But I shall not leave alone.'

'Who will go with you?'

The detective narrowed his eyes and answered with a smile.

'Why, the murderer, of course!'

The sound of voices came from the neighbouring room. Krag listened. 'They are talking about the dead man,' he said. 'Everybody is talking about him.'

He nodded to me and walked out of the door. He took his camera with him.

I lay for a while in my bed, collecting my thoughts. I hadn't the least desire to get up, but in the end, I leapt out from beneath the sheets and donned my light summer clothes. When I opened the windows, I found the warmth had returned, close and steamy. The sky hung low over the earth, and seemed to compress the air until it became thick with heat. Not a leaf was stirring: the wind from the night before had blown past long ago.

I stood there for a while, listening to the voices from the neighbouring room. The walls here are too damned thin, I thought. I stuck a cigarette in my mouth and left. My first question, once down in the lounge, was for the landlady. I asked for another room: the walls were too thin up there; I was disturbed by the voices around me. The landlady promised to arrange matters, and I went out to join the detective. I saw him straight away, in the shade beneath some big trees.

'Stop where you are,' he called out to me. 'Now I shall get an excellent shot of your profile.'

His camera snapped. He came towards me with a smile and begged my pardon.

'Amateur photography,' he said. 'It is my latest passion and since I am always excessive in my passions, I am, as an amateur photographer, a peril to my surroundings. You presented such a marvellous subject for a photograph against the brown rock; I do hope you can forgive me. Have you breakfasted?'

His questions came thick and fast.

'No,' I replied. 'Since it is so important for you to speak to me, I did not want to keep you waiting any longer.'

'I thought as much, I thought as much,' he murmured as he took me jovially by the arm. 'Come along and you shall see how I have arranged matters.'

He led me into one of the hotel's private rooms, where a breakfast table was laid for two. There were radishes and eggs, soft white bread, lobster, cold fish, a great quantity of light food

44

delightful in this summer heat, and cool, blue-white napkins. I fell into a good humour and thanked the detective for his thoughtful kindness.

'We shall talk all the better at a table such as this,' he said. 'I have a ravenous appetite. I have tramped about a great deal today.'

'So you arrived early, perhaps?'

'Half-past five by motorboat. I have already been to see the parson.'

'What in the world did you want with the parson?'

'Merely to ask him a simple question. He had no telephone, so I had to seek him out in person. I wanted to know if his horse had been driven out the night before last.'

I looked at the detective.

'So you must already have spoken to the fisherman, Jan Jansen, then?'

'Yes. Do you believe in this iron chariot?'

After a moment's thought, I replied. 'What a strange thing to ask. I'm quite taken aback by your question. How do you imagine a tolerably sensible man like me could believe in that fantastical old legend?'

'But you did hear the carriage rolling along, didn't you?'

'Yes.'

'A long way off?'

'Yes, a long, long way away. Yet I'd swear to it that the carriage I heard was rolling across the plain.'

'How would you describe the sound? Did it sound like the rattling of chains?'

'Almost. In any event, it certainly sounded very much like iron.'

'That is very interesting indeed,' muttered the detective. 'Would you be so good as to tell me all your experiences – from

45

the moment you saw the unfortunate forestry inspector in the garden of the great farm to the time you went to bed last night. In as much detail as possible, if you please.'

And so I told him all I knew. When I came to the discovery of the dead man, I forgot neither the ladies' terror nor the self-importance of the medical student as he played detective. 'Just imagine – he was sniffing around in the tracks,' I said. 'Apparently, he even measured the distance to the nearest tree.'

But these details seemed to be of no interest to the detective.

'Really,' he said, half-absently. 'Re…ally. Do carry on.'

When he heard about the hat, he asked: 'So the hat lay some distance away from the dead man?'

'Yes.'

'How far away?'

'I can't say precisely, but a few feet I would guess.'

When I had finished, Asbjørn Krag sat for a long time, sunk in thought.

'A most peculiar case,' he muttered.

'Indeed. I have got as far as yesterday evening now,' I said. 'But I still have one small thing to tell.'

The detective narrowed his eyes, and the sarcastic, sceptical expression spread across his face once more.

'What time did you go to bed last night?' he asked.

'Half-past one,' I replied.

'Then I know precisely what you are going to tell me. I dare say you heard the iron chariot again.'

I had nothing to say to this, because he had hit the mark.

A carriage was waiting down by the road. The detective shot a glance through the window.

'There's the police chief, come to fetch me,' he said. 'You must come along too.'

'Where to?'

'To the great farm. I have not been there yet. Don't you want to come?'

I thought it over.

'You must understand, of course,' I said, 'that I am somewhat shaken by yesterday's events. I would rather not be exposed to any fresh shocks.'

'What shocks could there be?' asked the detective. 'I am going to speak to the owner of Gjærnæs Farm. I simply want to hear a little about the unfortunate man's last visit there. You would be doing me a favour by accompanying me.'

'But I'm really not in the least bit interested in this case. Take the medical student along instead.'

But the detective seized me resolutely by the arm.

'Come along, now,' he said. 'You have no other business.'

The police chief treated the unknown detective with elaborate courtesy, even brushing off the seat of the carriage although it wasn't in the least bit dirty. When we drove away from the hotel, a large group of guests stood on the veranda watching us with great curiosity; the medical student came down towards us, clad in dazzling white sports clothes and eager to join us; but we drove away from him and left him standing there in disappointment, gazing after us with his hand shading his eyes. I waved to him ironically; he didn't strike me as very likeable – he was too handsome and besides, his handlebar moustache was too carefully groomed, and the smile beneath it always so secretive.

When we reached the sand-digger's hut, the police chief stopped the horse at Asbjørn Krag's request. Krag fiddled with his camera and asked the police chief to open the hut.

'What are you going to do in there?' I asked. 'Haven't you already seen the dead man?'

'Yes,' replied the detective. 'But there wasn't enough light then.'

'Enough light?'

'Yes, there wasn't enough light to take photographs – don't you understand?'

'But this is a breach of our agreement,' I objected. 'You guaranteed that I would not be exposed to any fresh shocks.'

The police chief was already drawing back the bolt on the door. Asbjørn Krag and I were standing alone by the carriage. And now that repulsive expression spread across the detective's face again, the narrow-eyed, sceptical look.

'Are you afraid of seeing him?' he asked. 'If so, you may wait outside here. I shall not oblige you to go in with me.'

Without answering, I walked quickly towards the hut. Asbjørn Krag followed me, still fiddling with his camera.

The little sand-digger's hut was not unlike those small dwellings built alongside railway works out in the wilderness. In its time, the hut had been used to store spades, pickaxes and other sand-digging tools. The walls were still lined with a number of these tools, coated in a crust of dried earth and clay.

There was only one room.

The detective threw open the window, filling the room with cool air from the plain. A broad, unplaned table stood in the middle of the room. Upon it lay the dead man.

I walked over to him and looked into his face. Now I recalled what the medical student had said the day before and was obliged to tacitly acknowledge that he had been right. The dead man appeared to be smiling, a smile that had a disdainful, almost triumphant air about it.

I started slightly at the snap of the detective's camera and when I looked around, I found the detective observing me sharply.

'I thought you were supposed to be photographing the dead

man,' I said.

'I am,' replied the detective. 'But I just had to take a picture of your face too. You had such an inimitable expression of wonder and dread. I have a positive mania for capturing emotion on the photographic plate.'

The detective moved the dead man so that the light fell upon his face. The forestry inspector now looked quite as though he were alive, for his cheeks were still suffused with the flush of the living. I stood and marvelled at his sharp, chiselled profile, with its high forehead. His hair was thick and brown, and I could see that it was combed over to the right. His beard had a reddish tinge.

'Shouldn't we straighten his tie?' I asked the detective. For the dead man's tie had been pushed backwards by his fall, causing the knot to ride up over one of his ears, and his stiff collar had snapped in two places.

'No,' said the detective sharply. 'Just leave him as he is.'

It seemed as if the detective would never be done photographing the dead man. The air in the room became steadily more oppressive and I felt ill at ease but did not wish the detective to notice my weakness. In the end, he finished, but by the time he had folded up all his equipment, I was close to fainting.

Asbjørn Krag opened the door, letting a draught sweep through the room. It seemed to do me good. I could see that the police chief had become a little pale too. He had never had anything to do with a case like this before. Asbjørn Krag, on the other hand, was as calm as ever, as unchangeable. He put new plates into his camera, whistling all the while. It seemed that the dead man lying on the table was no more to him than an interesting photographic subject.

'Shall we drive on, then?' I asked.

'Not yet,' he replied. 'First I want to look at the hat.'

He picked up the dead man's hat, placed it on his fingertips and examined it intently, as if he were at a gentlemen's outfitters choosing himself some new headgear.

'Do you remember,' he asked me, 'how he was wearing his hat the last time you saw him?'

'The way anybody would generally wear a green hunting hat, no differently,' I replied.

The detective appeared entirely indifferent to my displeasure at his lingering so long in this chamber of death.

'Just let me see,' he muttered, and without further ado, he pulled the green hunting hat down over my head.

'Like that, yes,' he continued his monologue. He adjusted the hat slightly. 'That's how it must have sat… That is exceptionally interesting. Are you feeling uncomfortable?' he asked.

'My nerves are not made of steel,' I replied. 'Look at the police chief, he isn't so comfortable either.'

'On the contrary,' the police chief was quick to say. 'I just felt that the air in here was a little…a little close and stifling.'

'Yes, well we're finished now. I do apologise for being so slow.'

The detective laid a hand upon my shoulder; narrowing his eyes until they became two black slits behind his pince-nez, he said, 'You are right. Your nerves are certainly not made of steel.'

He placed the green hunting hat back on the dead man's breast, and all three of us left the sand-digger's hut. The police chief drew the bolt on the door.

It felt tremendously liberating to walk out over the open plain, to breathe in fresh air beneath the high, blue sky. During our absence, the horse had grazed its way further and further from the country road, dragging the wheels of the carriage down into the ditch. It took the strength of three men to lift the carriage back up onto the road again. And so we drove on towards Gjærnæs. It was two o'clock.

The detective appeared to have a feeling for the beauty of the landscape, too. He framed the forest and the tarns with his hands, as if composing a picture, and said, 'What a subject for a painter!'

It was astonishing that he could think of such matters when his thoughts should have been occupied by the strange and sinister mystery he had undertaken to solve.

We were approaching Gjærnæs Farm. Out in the fields, work was in full swing. As we drove by, people straightened up and shaded their eyes. Asbjørn Krag also admired the fine, leafy avenue that led up to the farm; at the end of this fragrant tunnel, we could see the white façade of the farm itself and as we drove past the garden, our gaze was met by a riot of colour, clusters of lilac blossom swaying between the chalk-white staves of the fence. All the doors and windows in the main building were open, and the wind coursed freely through the house, drawing the curtains in with it. There was a heavy scent of meadows and grain and growing clover; it was a beautiful bright summer's day beneath a wide-open sky.

The police chief halted the horse with a tug of the reins, causing the hot gravel to crunch beneath its hooves. We sat in the carriage and stared at the front door, to see if anybody would come, and eventually, a bareheaded man in a white summer jacket filled the doorway. It was the steward; I nodded and jumped out of the carriage.

'Master home?' I asked.

'Yes.'

The man did not move, but stood with his hands in his trouser pockets, staring at us with curiosity.

'We would rather speak to Gjærnæs himself,' I said, and walked towards him.

51

'You'd best come in, then,' answered the steward, without stepping aside from the doorway.

I looked at him more closely now. It was the same man as the other night, the steward who had denied me entry to the house. He was still very pale, I could see it quite clearly. His eyes squinted narrowly, prompting thoughts of sleepless nights, and there was something greyish and yellow and thin-nosed about his pallor – as always happens with coarse, robust people who are seized by a deep grief or suffer some intense fright.

At last, the man set his thick soles in motion. He led us into one of the parlours. The detective placed his camera case upon the table and at once set about observing the steward. He looked at him for a long time. Astonished by his curiosity, the steward asked: 'Who's this fellow?'

'I am from Kristiania,' replied Krag. 'I am a detective.'

Once again, Krag gazed searchingly at the man, adding, 'And you are the steward here, are you not?'

'Yes.'

The steward turned away, muttering that he should alert his master. Understandably enough, he had become embarrassed and when he reached the door, he turned back once more but vanished swiftly on meeting Asbjørn Krag's gaze again.

A peculiar smile crept over the detective's mouth. He had stationed himself by the window and was sitting with his back to the light. His eyes were downcast, and it seemed to me that he was observing the straw hat that lay on his knee with excessive interest. Otherwise, he sat quite still. The police chief was standing over by the window, keeping an eye on the horse. Somewhere inside the house, a woman's voice spoke angrily, and the sound of a bicycle bell floated in from the road outside. Nobody came.

'Did you notice the steward?' I asked.

'Yes,' answered the detective enquiringly, as if what he actually meant to say was: 'What of it?'

'Did you notice his face? It seemed to me that he was pretty unhappy.'

'Ah...ha.'

'You should talk to him.'

'Ah...ha... Why?'

'Perhaps he knows something.'

'What would he know?'

His question confused me. I did not pursue the conversation any further. Eventually, we heard footsteps in the adjoining room – we had been waiting for more than ten minutes by that time – and a man came in.

It was Gjærnæs himself, a heavily built man in his forties. He nodded amiably to me and shook my hand, and when Asbjørn Krag was introduced to him, he wished us all welcome.

He asked the detective simply: 'I dare say you've come about the murder?'

Asbjørn Krag assented. Gjærnæs nodded thoughtfully and murmured, half to himself, 'Well, well. What peculiar experiences life sends one's way.'

His whole demeanour in that instant was so remarkable that I was quite struck with astonishment. The thought ran through my head: what on earth must Asbjørn Krag think? He has come here to solve a mysterious murder. All the people he has met so far have expressed only repulsion and horror for the crime itself; but now he comes to this farm where he is expecting to obtain information about the unfortunate man's activities in the final hours before his death. First he meets the farm steward, whose wretched and dejected appearance must astonish him; and now the owner of the farm himself behaves in such a way as to utterly convince one that he has recently been struck by some great and irremediable misfortune. I have never seen a man so dispirited, so deeply unhappy as Gjærnæs. It would take very little more to give a stranger the distinct suspicion that the people at the farm – both owner and steward – knew more about the crime than the rest of us. Asbjørn Krag looked at him in surprise. Gjærnæs paced back and forth across the room in front of the detective. He tried to gain mastery of himself, struggled his way to some kind of composure and then stood quite motionless in the middle of the room – not a quiver of his fingertips, nor a flicker of his eyelids. I am familiar with this state myself, where the very nervousness that overwhelms you also brings you to calm, though all the while your nerve-ends burn like glowing fibres.

'Forestry Inspector Blinde left here at eleven o'clock the evening before last,' began the detective. 'He was seen at the hotel at nine o'clock. So we have reason to believe that he was with you for an hour and a half. Is that correct?'

'Yes, that is correct.'

'What was the purpose of his visit?'

'He came on important business.'

'Very important?'

'Yes. He came to ask for my sister's hand in marriage.'

This answer was followed by an oppressive silence that lasted many seconds.

And then Asbjørn Krag asked again, 'Was Blinde happy when he left, or unhappy?'

'I assume,' replied Gjærnæs, 'that he was very happy indeed, because he loved my sister dearly and she had promised to marry him.'

I did not wait to see how the detective would pursue the conversation, but broke in, 'Before he left you, did he by any chance mention having enemies?'

'It occurs to me that he did mention something of the sort.'

From the side, Asbjørn Krag looked at me enquiringly but allowed me to continue with my questions.

'Did he mention any names?'

'No, he did not. He was so happy and contented that the thought of his enemies only clouded his mood quite fleetingly. I remember that he exclaimed as he was leaving: 'Just think how many will envy me. Ah, now I shall have made some terrible enemies.''

'Did you consent to the match?' asked Krag.

'Yes, of course,' replied Gjærnæs.

'Why of course?'

'Because it is what she wanted. It would never cross my mind to oppose her wishes.'

'Then I shall ask you a more direct question,' continued Asbjørn Krag. 'Were you happy with this match?'

'No,' replied Gjærnæs solemnly.

'Why not?'

'Because I did not like Forestry Inspector Blinde, of course. I did not think him a pleasant man. He always struck me as supercilious and arrogant, and he did not improve on closer acquaintance. Even after he had won my sister's hand, I found him somewhat repulsive. There was something triumphant about him.'

Suddenly Asbjørn Krag pricked up his ears.

'Would you use that word,' he asked, 'triumphant?'

'Yes, it occurred to me...'

'But one can use it in different senses. Do you mean triumphant because he had attained the happiness of becoming engaged to your sister? Or egotistically triumphant, because it was he and not one of his rivals who had that happiness?'

'I mean egotistically triumphant. There was always something egotistical about him.'

'Were you surprised when you heard about the calamity?'

'Surprised is far too mild a way of putting it,' replied Gjærnæs. 'I was horrified.'

'And your sister?'

'She has spent the whole day weeping. She has just this minute gone to bed because she feels so crushed, so ill.'

'I would very much like to speak to her.'

Suddenly Gjærnæs became so uneasy that he started to stammer.

'That is quite impossible,' he said. 'She has gone to bed.'

Asbjørn Krag made no reply. But all at once he developed a remarkable interest in the room's fittings. It was quite low ceilinged, as so many of these big old farmhouses are. The furniture was old, the chairs upholstered in a pale, striped fabric.

'I am terribly fond of wandering around old farmhouses,' remarked the detective as he got up. 'Would you permit me to take a look at the other rooms, Mr Gjærnæs?'

'Yes, gladly, although you come at a slightly inconvenient time,' replied Gjærnæs. 'We are in the middle of the summer work and have no time to keep things tidy.'

'That doesn't matter.'

The detective looked out of the window. He nodded in satisfaction. There in the farmyard stood the steward, holding the horse's reins, even though it was quite unnecessary; the steward was chatting to the horse, which twitched its ears and shook away the flies. It was my distinct belief that the steward was waiting there for the detective's return.

Gjærnæs now took us about the old rooms and Asbjørn Krag inspected everything with interest, questioned and queried this and that, wanted to know all about how old the furniture was and who the people in the family portraits were. Above Gjærnæs's writing-desk hung a bromide enlargement of a photograph. It showed an old man with a goatee beard, small sharp eyes and a crooked nose.

'Who is that?' asked Krag.

'My father,' replied Gjærnæs gruffly.

I tried to signal to the detective that he should not enquire any further because I had remembered the fisherman's tale about the old man's tragic end. But either the detective failed to notice my gesture or he chose not to pay attention to it.

'Is he dead?' he asked.

'Yes,' replied Gjærnæs, as he opened the door to the next room.

'How did he die?'

'It was a sudden death,' muttered Gjærnæs.

'Aha, sudden…hmmm.'

The detective stood looking at the photograph, but when Gjærnæs began to speak feverishly of other matters he was obliged to tear himself away from it.

Gjærnæs also showed us his sister's rooms.

'But she isn't here after all!' exclaimed Asbjørn Krag in astonishment.

'I beg your pardon?'

'You said she had gone to bed.'

'Yes, indeed. But she is resting in another room.'

Gjærnæs stared into her sun-filled apartment.

'She is lying in a room on the shady side of the house,' he said.

'Ah, is that so?'

We went on and came to Gjærnæs's library. He was a great reader. A thick blind was drawn tightly down over the room's single window, so it was fairly dark in there.

'And now I have nothing more to show you,' said Gjærnæs.

'What about that door?' asked Asbjørn Krag, pointing to a double door across the room. 'Where does that lead to?'

Gjærnæs stood protectively in front of it.

'That is where my sister is sleeping,' he said.

I gave an involuntary start. Once again, there was a ring of hopelessness and despondency in the man's voice, and I was reminded of the incident on the night of the murder, when the steward had so zealously refused me entry to the house.

I do not know whether Asbjørn Krag noticed the change in our host's behaviour; in any event, it appeared not to make the slightest impression on him. His thoughts had returned to the murder. As we slowly drifted through the rooms, going back the way we had come, he asked: 'Do you have any inkling who the murderer might be?'

Gjærnæs stopped, and leaned on the back of a chair.

'I have no idea,' he replied.

'And your sister?'

'It is a mystery to her too.'

'And have you no information of value to the investigation?'

'No, on the contrary. All the information I can offer about the unfortunate man's visit here serves only to increase the mystery of the whole affair.'

'You are right,' replied Asbjørn Krag.

When we were taking our leave of Gjærnæs, the detective said, 'But then there is the chariot.'

Gjærnæs did not understand.

'The chariot?' he asked.

'Yes, didn't you know?' replied Asbjørn Krag. 'The iron chariot was heard on the night of the murder.'

Our host smiled – a peculiar, strained smile.

'That old legend,' he muttered. 'Yes, of course, that old legend would come up again now; people do have such lively imaginations. What do you think about the iron chariot, Mr Detective?'

'I do not believe in ghosts,' replied Asbjørn Krag. 'But people have heard a carriage rolling across this desolate plain, that much is certain.'

'Yes, but what of it?'

'Well, then there must naturally have been a vehicle – not some ghostly chariot but an ordinary carriage. You, the parson and the police chief are the only people for dozens of miles around here who have horses. The parson's horse did not drive out that night and neither did the police chief's.'

'Nor mine, either,' replied Gjærnæs hastily.

Just then, through the open window, he caught sight of the steward, who was standing in the farmyard, helping the police chief's horse keep off the flies.

He raised a hand to his brow and suddenly seemed oddly agitated.

'You have a long drive ahead of you,' he mumbled – although the drive ahead of us was far from long. 'Perhaps you'd best give your horse some oats.'

The police chief protested in confusion and said there was no need.

But Gjærnæs hurried out into the farmyard and we followed.

It now became clear to one and all that the matter of the oats was merely a pretext – God knows why, but it was in any event terribly obvious. Gjærnæs went up to the steward and whispered a few hasty words to him, scratching the horse's muzzle so frantically all the while that it tossed its head and bared its white teeth. The police chief and I both saw it; only Asbjørn Krag had all at once become absorbed by something else entirely. With a smile, he was observing a little black and white rat terrier as it came growling towards us – its eyes glaring angrily over a snout as round and black as the muzzle of a rifle.

At last we climbed into the carriage. Asbjørn Krag waved goodbye to Gjærnæs.

'Farewell,' he shouted. 'I hope we meet again. I am staying at the hotel.'

But as he said this, he looked at the steward, who lowered his gaze.

As we drove along the avenue, I said, 'I don't understand why you didn't question the steward too.'

'What about?'

'Why, about whether any of Gjærnæs's horses had been out that night, of course.'

'I thought it quite unnecessary,' replied the detective.

We drove out onto the plain.

Asbjørn Krag shoved his straw hat down over his eyes to shade them from the sun, which was blazing mercilessly. In front of his knees dangled the inevitable black camera case.

He was silent for quite some time, but I had a feeling that he was sitting thinking beneath his straw hat.

At length, he asked: 'What did he die of?'

'Who?'

'The old man. The father.'

'He drowned.'

'So he wasn't killed then?' asked the detective.

'No,' I replied.

IV

The Steward

FOR SOME DAYS, NOTHING OF SIGNIFICANCE happened. The strange mystery up on the plain cast a sinister atmosphere over the place and several of the summer guests left the hotel. Indeed I was supposed to have left too, but Asbjørn Krag urged me to stay. He claimed I could be of assistance to him. The medical student, who secretly nursed a passion for the art of policing, was green with envy because Asbjørn Krag would have nothing to do with him. But how I could be of service to him – that I truly did not understand. So far, at any rate, I had not helped him; quite the contrary. I had sometimes expressed myself ironically on the subject of his working methods. I found them quite peculiar and hardly worthy of a tireless detective. His days slipped by in calm idleness; he would sleep until late in the morning, eat heartily at all meals, bathe and go for long walks. In short, he behaved entirely like a holidaying gentleman. If anybody questioned him, he would give either an evasive answer or none at all, then simply stare at the questioner with his sarcastic, narrowed eyes. He met people's myriad hypotheses about the motive for the crime with absolute indifference, irrespective of whether they were circulated by the summer guests, the villagers or the local policemen. He would listen patiently and when the informant concluded with the words, 'So I believe this or that,' Asbjørn Krag would merely respond in his most indifferent tone: 'Aha… aa.'

Or he might say: 'Yes, indeed. Hmmm. I see.'

But whenever anybody asked him, 'What is your opinion, though, sir?' he would answer, as if astonished by the question: 'Me? Why, I simply haven't had time to form an opinion yet.'

God knows what he was actually up to. As far as I could tell, he was no longer conducting even the most minimal of investigations. When by chance he met Gjærnæs, the owner of the great farm, on one of his excursions, he spoke to him about the outlook for the annual harvest. One day, black patches appeared among the bright clusters of summer guests. It was the family of the dead man, come to arrange for his body to be sent home; but the crepe veils and the white kerchiefs tucked into black gloves quickly vanished again. Krag had not even troubled to pay his respects to the family – and then everything was as it had been before.

In the meantime, the police chief and the other local policemen were working independently of the detective. The police chief cycled and drove and rushed about terribly, but without coming an inch closer to solving the mystery, of course. The question of theft could now no longer be ruled out, since it emerged that the forestry inspector had been in possession of a sum of money at the time of his death – some several hundred kroner. Furthermore, he owned a green wallet made of pressed alligator skin. Neither wallet nor money had been found on the body. True enough, the fact that both his gold watch and his ring had still been in his possession weighed against the robbery hypothesis; even so, the police circulated a description of some tinkers who might conceivably have been staying in the vicinity at the time of the murder.

But Asbjørn Krag's idleness and indifference eased the atmosphere; little by little the agitation and nervousness subsided and summertime life slipped back into its accustomed rut; gloomy whispers and secretive conversations in hushed tones gave way to happy laughter and chat along the roads, and the sea rang once again with the irregular oar-strokes of the seaside guests.

The reader will no doubt recall that on the morning of Asbjørn Krag's arrival, I had asked to be given a different room. By chance I had discovered that the hotel carried sound as effectively as a telephone wire, and I have always found it annoying to be unable to speak in one room without being heard in the rooms to left and right. But there were no more rooms free at the hotel just then, so the landlady sniffed one out for me that lay just a few minutes' walk away, out on a little spit of land called Kobbeodden. I was now staying there quite alone, in a little cabin, although I still ate at the hotel.

The first day after my move, the detective asked me, 'Aren't you afraid to live in such a lonely spot?'

'No. Why ever should I be afraid?' I answered.

'The nights are still light for now,' said Asbjørn Krag, peering up at the sky. 'But the dark nights will be here presently.'

'I don't understand you.'

'So this sinister business has not affected your nerves, then?'

'No.'

'Good. Then you're just the man to assist me. I hope you'll be staying a few days longer.'

'I shall gladly stay a few days more,' I replied. 'And I don't think it will be any hardship for me to assist you.'

'Oh, really?'

'For I cannot see that you are doing anything at all.'

Asbjørn Krag smiled and then he said something that astonished me greatly at the time, but that I would recall on a later occasion. He said, 'But you must concede that time is passing.'

'What do you actually do all day?' I asked.

'I write letters,' he replied. 'And I have put some agents in Kristiania to a great deal of trouble gathering information. And then, I am waiting – for something that will happen.'

'Will happen?'

'Yes.'

On just that occasion, I was on my way back to my little cabin out on the headland, and Asbjørn Krag had accompanied me. He harboured a peculiar interest in this cabin of mine. He said it reminded him of a little lighthouse, standing as it did, right at the end of the headland.

As we were approaching the cabin, he pointed to it and said, 'Do you see now how lonely your place is?'

'I certainly am staying in a lonely spot.'

'Here we are, beside the house nearest to your own cabin, and it is still several minutes' walk from here down to your place.'

'Yes, I realise that.'

The detective shook his head thoughtfully and walked on.

He left me by the wall of the cabin.

Before he went, I asked him, 'Do you give any credence to that theory about the tinkers?'

'Well, you know,' he said. 'I hardly think Forestry Inspector Blinde is likely to have greeted any tinkers that crossed his path that night.'

I looked at him nonplussed.

'Greet…?'

'Why yes,' he continued, and now, for once, he was genuinely animated. 'Forestry Inspector Blinde was dealt that mortal blow as he was greeting somebody.'

'How can you possibly maintain that?'

'There are several things that clearly imply it. Do you remember the hat? It lay a couple of paces away from the body. It was quite undamaged and yet the fatal blow was to the back of Blinde's head. If the hat had been on his head at that moment, it would also have shown signs of the terrible blow. But he was holding the hat in his hand, he was greeting somebody.'

'Who was he greeting?'

'The murderer,' answered Asbjørn Krag. 'And at that very moment, the murderer struck him.'

'What an astonishing thing to say,' I replied after a moment's thought. 'You may well be right.'

'I am right. In other words, the murderer was one of the forestry inspector's acquaintances. He was one of the enemies Blinde had spoken of when he left Gjærnæs that evening.'

This was the first time Asbjørn Krag's conversation had indicated to me that he was thinking about the drama and drawing conclusions. So I seized the moment and questioned him eagerly, for he seemed suddenly to be in a communicative frame of mind. I asked if he had found any other clues, whether he could think who the criminal might be, or at least what social class he might belong to.

But the detective would not be drawn any deeper into the matter; he brushed me aside, and returned once again to the question of my cabin's isolated location.

'Farewell,' I said.

'Farewell,' he replied. 'I shall go back to my room to wait.'

'What is it you're actually waiting for?'

Instead of answering, he looked at me with an odd expression on his face, and asked, 'Do you believe in the power that can lie in a pair of eyes?'

'Are you talking about hypnotism?'

'Well, you may call it hypnotism if you wish. I have used my eyes to make a person come to me. That is the person I am waiting for.'

He would not explain any further and walked away from me slowly. I stood looking after him and marvelling at his strange behaviour. Suddenly, he squatted down, holding his camera in front of him. What did he intend to photograph now – nothing but the shining sea? The sun struck sparks off the white stones around him. Perhaps he had found a subject after all: tufts of grass and seaweed protruded here and there, and a few small skerries were left bare and glistening when the sea drew back. Then a calm swell would rise up and close over it all, like a vast lip. Krag snapped, then got up and strolled off. A peculiar soul.

At around eight, I went down to the hotel to eat supper. I met Asbjørn Krag along the way.

'I have something to tell you,' he said at once. 'The man has arrived.'

'I don't know who you are talking about.'

Asbjørn Krag took me by the arm in an access of joviality and said, 'You remember what I said to you a short while ago about the power of the eyes? Good. I used my gaze to summon somebody here to me. This is the person I have been awaiting for the past few days. You know him too, and right now he is sitting up in my room.'

And now I recalled the detective's parting with Gjærnæs; the way he had said to the owner, while looking at the steward: 'I hope we meet again. I am staying at the hotel.'

'It must be the steward at Gjærnæs Farm who has arrived,' I said.

'Correctly deduced,' answered the detective. 'I would like you to hear our conversation, and that is why I came to find you.'

I was greatly struck by his words.

'So there is some connection between Gjærnæs and the murder, after all?' I murmured. 'Good heavens, when I think what you told me earlier – about the murdered man's hat.'

'He had doffed his hat in greeting when he was dealt that terrible blow.'

'Yes, and remember what Gjærnæs himself said: that he was quite opposed to the marriage between Blinde and his sister. Perhaps Gjærnæs hated Blinde; he said himself that he found Blinde unpleasant and egotistical.'

'Egotistically triumphant,' the detective corrected me.

'Indeed. But the main point is that the murderer knew Blinde. I tremble with suspense at the thought of hearing what the steward has to say.'

Asbjørn Krag shook his head and squinted at me with narrowed, sarcastic eyes.

'Now you are too eager,' he said slowly, as if soothing. 'You are getting ahead of yourself, my dear fellow.'

'I am merely connecting the different elements,' I replied.

'Tell me, then, what conclusions you reach.'

'Gjærnæs was opposed to the marriage.'

'Quite so, but he still gave his consent, because it was his sister's wish.'

'But he was strongly opposed to it at any rate. And he didn't like Blinde. If he expressed himself so strongly even to us, we may perhaps deduce that he hated the forestry inspector.'

'Before you go any further, I would like to ask you outright,' said Krag, 'whether you believe Gjærnæs to be the murderer.'

I shuddered at this dreadful question.

'I don't want to make any horrible accusations,' I answered. 'You asked me to present a series of conclusions. It strikes me as an affectation on your part to deny that some circumstances point directly towards Gjærnæs. I also presume that you have already formed your own opinion. I do not believe Gjærnæs to be the guilty party, but if we gather together all the elements that count against him it may be easier for us to save him from this terrible suspicion. Gjærnæs is my friend.'

The detective still had me by the arm. He slowed his pace so that we would not arrive at the hotel too soon. I suddenly had the impression that he very much wished to hear my opinion – and, remarkably enough, he once again raised Gjærnæs's name directly in connection with the crime.

'We must not just consider evidence,' he said. 'We must also look at it in human terms. Can you envisage the possibility that Gjærnæs might do something of this nature?'

After thinking for a while, I replied: 'With difficulty.'

'Put yourself in his place,' continued the detective. 'You have a sister of whom you are exceedingly fond.'

'And whom I look up to.'

'Very well. She declares that she is willing to marry a man whom you hate.'

'The reason I hate him is, of course, that I know him to be a bad person.'

'Naturally. You try to convince your beloved sister to break off the engagement; but the object of your hatred is a very handsome man, and she is blinded by passionate love. You understand that the marriage is a mistake and that your sister will be deeply unhappy, but you see that there is no point trying to convince her. She gives the hated man her consent and then comes the moment when the lover reveals himself to

68

be 'egotistically triumphant'. I like the expression that Gjærnæs unwittingly let slip. I imagine that Blinde knew of the brother's opposition to the match, and that he made a great show of his egotistical triumph once he had obtained the sister's consent. And now put yourself in Gjærnæs's place. Can you not imagine how, in the heat of the moment – seeing Blinde's triumphant, disdainful smile and knowing your beloved sister to be at the mercy of this terrible person – you might be tempted to kill him?'

Asbjørn Krag spoke urgently, and I found myself strangely gripped by his words.

'I suppose so,' I replied, uncertainly, '...I suppose so. But naturally I would not have done it on purpose.'

'Naturally. You would have acted in the heat of the moment, seized by a sudden burst of violent anger or embittered dejection. Let us say that you met him on a deserted road; that he greeted you and smiled at you sarcastically, triumphantly as if to say: "Now you can see, my friend; now I have your dear sister in my power, she is mine" – how far do you go now, driven by all that hatred of yours... What then? I do believe you might strike him, perhaps not thinking to kill him but merely overcome by an insurmountable urge to knock him down... But what is on your mind? Aren't you enjoying this conversation of ours?'

I wiped the sweat from my forehead. I felt my lips begin to grow cold.

'I was thinking of the dead man,' I stammered. 'Do you remember his face? It was just as maliciously triumphant as you say. And I am also thinking about the disturbed behaviour of my dear friend Gjærnæs; he was pale and tremulous, and looked as if he had not slept for several days. And then the steward... So now he has come to you. What has he got to say?'

'That is what we shall find out now,' replied the detective.

We went up to his room. When we walked in, the steward got up and greeted us diffidently. He was in his Sunday best but, other than that, there was no change to remark in him: the same despondency of manner, the same uncertain, shifty look.

'You know my friend,' said the detective. 'He is assisting me in my investigations. He would also like to hear what you have to say.'

'Very well,' the steward assented simply, with enormous gravity. He did not know quite how to begin; he was quiet and dispirited.

'I have something to tell you,' he continued after a while. 'But it's so hard for me to know how to come out with it. Could you ask me some questions?'

'You wish, perhaps, to speak of the murder?'

'No, I don't know anything about the murder.' He looked to one side timidly. 'I don't know anything about that. And I don't want to tell you about anything but what I saw with my own eyes.'

'We do not wish to hear about anything else, either,' the detective replied.

The steward nodded in my direction.

'Do you remember that night when I wouldn't let you in?'

'Yes,' I said. 'It seemed to me that you were a little brutal on that occasion.'

'Brutal, yes, but I had to be. That was the night it all started.'

'What started?'

'All that mysterious commotion at the farm. It's a great shame it should happen now, when we've been living peacefully for so many years. I don't mind telling you I'm very fond of Gjærnæs. He's cleverer and nicer and less bad-tempered than the old man was.'

Asbjørn Krag interrupted him here: 'You mean Gjærnæs's

70

late father?'

'Yes.'

This prompted the detective to return to the long-forgotten death.

'Is it known for a fact that he drowned?' he asked.

'Yes,' replied the steward. 'He drowned. The boat drifted ashore, capsized, out among the skerries… Yes, it began that night, as I said,' he continued. 'A man came with a letter for Gjærnæs and after reading it, he rushed through the rooms like a madman, calling out for the mistress.'

'Do you know where the letter was from?'

'No, I don't. But I was in Gjærnæs's office when it arrived. It was in a large yellow envelope.'

'Did you see the writing?'

'No, but when Gjærnæs saw the writing on the envelope he came over a bit peculiar straight away.'

'Did he say anything?'

'Yes, he said: Good God, I have never seen anything like this… Then he opened the letter and read it. And after reading the first few lines, he came close to fainting, or at any rate he went awfully pale; yes, he sat there in his chair as pale as a corpse. The oddest thing I've ever seen.'

'You say that he ran through the rooms?'

'Yes, that was after he'd pulled himself together. But first he threw me out. "You must not stay here any longer," he said. "Damn it all, you must not stay here any longer." He didn't wait for me to leave but rushed through the rooms almost out of his mind, calling out for the mistress.'

'Was she at home?'

'Yes, she was.'

'What did he say to her?'

'That I don't know. I left. Later the maids told me the mistress had cried out, but then she'd tried to soothe Gjærnæs. The two of them talked together in the library for a long time, with all the doors and windows shut tight. After that, I was called in. "Now listen to me, my dear steward," said Gjærnæs. "I received a surprising letter a short time ago. In one sense it was most distressing, but in another it was also very joyous. In any event, I was greatly moved when I read it, and I wish to ask you to forget this incident and not speak of it to a soul. It concerns a quite private matter. There is nothing more to speak of." I didn't believe a word of it, though, because my master was still quite pale.'

'When did this happen?'

'At around nine in the evening.'

'Before Forestry Inspector Blinde came, then?'

'Yes, half an hour before. When he arrived, Gjærnæs wanted to turn him away at first, but the mistress let him in. The three of them had a long conversation together. It was towards the end of this conversation that you arrived.'

Here, the steward nodded towards me.

'The mistress saw you through the window,' he continued. 'She ran out to me and asked me not to let you in under any circumstances. Gjærnæs himself came out too and cried out as if he were losing his wits. "I must be alone," he shouted. "Can't you see that I am sick?" That is why I had to be so brutal with you, there was no other reason.'

'Did you hear absolutely nothing of what was said?' asked the detective.

'No, nothing much. But at one point I heard the mistress chiding Gjærnæs. "You should be happy," she said. "And instead you are in mortal despair".'

'What did he say to that?'

'He said: "Of course I'm happy, Hilde, but this is terrible all

72

the same. How are we to keep it a secret?" But I also heard him say something else.'

The detective asked no further questions. I understood that we had now reached a crucial point in the steward's strange tale.

'He said something else,' the steward repeated, in a low, almost whispering voice. 'And I couldn't help hearing it because I was walking through the rooms just then. Gjærnæs said: "But he is doomed."'

The detective listened to this with a poker face.

'To whom did he say this?' he asked.

'To the mistress.'

'Why not to Forestry Inspector Blinde, who was also there?'

'Blinde was not with them at that moment; he was waiting in the mistress's apartment. Miss Hilde and Gjærnæs were alone in the study.'

'Do you have any idea whom Gjærnæs was referring to?'

'How could I?'

Again, the steward's gaze shifted timidly to one side.

'You may well have your own thoughts on the matter,' he said. 'The same night, that terrible thing happened out on the plain. Forestry Inspector Blinde left the farm at eleven o'clock.'

Asbjørn Krag sat for a long time in silence; his next question went straight to the heart of the matter: 'But how can Gjærnæs have anything to do with this murder? He stayed at the farm, did he not?'

The steward did not reply. He sat with bowed head, fiddling diffidently with his hat. Presently, he muttered: 'I hadn't intended to come to you. But then I happened to hear something. I heard from some other people that you were going around asking about a horse…or a carriage.'

'Yes, I would like to find out if any of the local people drove out that night.'

73

The steward looked up.

'And I suppose there wasn't anybody, was there?'

'No, neither the police chief nor the parson.'

'Or Gjærnæs?'

'Not Gjærnæs, either.'

There was a long pause.

The detective asked, 'What was it Gjærnæs said to you when we drove away from the farm that day?'

'I'm sure you can guess for yourself,' replied the steward. 'He told me to hold my tongue; the same thing he's said to me every single day now since that letter came.'

'But what were you to hold your tongue about?'

After a long while, the steward managed to stammer out an answer.

'Gjærnæs…he actually did drive out on the night of the murder.'

I expected Asbjørn Krag to leap up on hearing these momentous words. But he simply sat there quite placidly, as if nothing had happened. And his calm irritated me; a terrible sinister feeling stole over me – I felt an urge to walk out across the meadows cooling my hot face in the summer wind; but I just sat there, as if paralysed, my nerves aquiver. I felt an urge to say something, too, to ask something, but I dared not open my mouth for fear of my own voice – there was such a painful weight in my throat that perhaps I might be unable to get the words out. And there sat this man, smiling, eyes almost shut, cool as a cucumber; at that moment, I found him repulsive and almost hated him, because I knew that I could not guess a single one of his thoughts. What was he thinking about? What did he believe now? And he was speaking in such an infuriatingly normal way, too, with such seeming indifference.

'So Gjærnæs actually did drive out that night. Aha.'

'Yes,' replied the steward. 'And nobody on the farm knew about it but me. As soon as the forestry inspector left, Gjærnæs asked me to quietly hitch up the horse because he wanted to go out for a drive. It was odd, you know, because why in the world would he want to drive out so late at night? And nobody else was to know about it, either. Quietly as possible, I led the horse out to the back of the farm, and hitched it up to an old cart we keep standing there.'

'Why did you use that cart in particular?'

'I couldn't go into the cart shed because that would've woken everybody up, and then how could I keep it a secret that the master was going out for a drive?'

'Did he drive out alone?'

'All alone. I offered to go with him, but that sent him into a panic. "Are you mad?" he said. I had to promise him I'd go to bed and not worry about his return. Gjærnæs drove out across the plain and I stood watching him until he'd disappeared into the darkness. Then I went to bed.'

'Did you sleep?'

'No, I couldn't. I lay awake all night long and thought about what I'd seen and heard. I knew something odd must have happened. The master looked terrible when he drove off, as if he was drunk. But he hadn't had a drop, I know that for a fact.'

'Did you hear him come back again?'

'Yes, I heard thuds and noises from the stalls when he was stabling the horse.'

'The cart he drove out in – what was it like?'

'A rattling old buggy.'

'An iron chariot?'

The steward smiled. 'I know what you're after,' he replied. 'I've heard that old legend too, but I don't believe in ghosts. The old buggy might rattle a bit, but it's still very difficult to tell it apart from any other carriage when you hear it from a distance.'

'So it isn't the one I've heard, then?' I interjected, eagerly.

'Oh yes,' the steward replied with a smile. 'It probably is the one you've heard.'

I said nothing.

The detective asked, 'But haven't you seen or heard anything odd on the farm since that night?'

'That's just it, I have. The farm has a secret. It seems as if peculiar things are going on at all hours of the day and night. Gjærnæs and Miss Hilde are both quite different from the way they used to be.'

'What did you think when you heard about the murder?'

'I didn't think anything,' muttered the steward. 'But when I heard you were going round asking about the carriage, it went against my conscience to keep quiet about what I knew.'

'I knew you would come,' said the detective.

'You looked at me so strangely when you left Gjærnæs,' said the steward. 'I didn't dare wait any longer.'

He got up.

'And I don't reckon I've done anything wrong,' he continued. 'I told the master I was coming to visit you.'

'Did he try to stop you?'

'Yes, and when he realised it was no use, he said everything that had happened concerned him personally.'

Asbjørn Krag sat there for a long time, deep in thought.

'You may go back to the farm,' he said eventually.

'Very well.'

'And you may send my greetings to Gjærnæs and ask when it would be convenient for him to receive me.'

'Convenient!' I cried, in astonishment.

Asbjørn Krag held up an admonishing hand and continued to address the steward.

'And you may tell him, furthermore, that I shall not intrude upon his secrets.'

Shortly afterwards, the farm steward departed, leaving me alone with Asbjørn Krag.

'So what do you think?' he asked.

'It seems to me that Gjærnæs is done for,' I replied. 'What a terrible misfortune though, poor fellow!'

But Asbjørn Krag's thoughts must have been a long way away off, for he said absent-mindedly, 'Done for, aha. So that's what you think, is it?'

He became ever more taciturn and when I realised that he wished to be left alone with his broodings, I took my leave.

I came late to the supper table and it was eleven o'clock before I had finished eating. When I went past his window, I heard him pacing back and forth inside and so, not wishing to disturb him, I took the road home to my little cabin. A storm was brewing and although the evening had so far been mild and summer bright, a rainstorm was now blustering away somewhere out on the horizon, making the air damp and gusty; it arrived in an instant, like breath upon a shining metal plate. The sea turned up its lead-grey belly in the harbour. It had been dead calm for several hours, but now the sea far out on the horizon was crashing, forming a black furrow, and the wind and rain were moving ever closer.

I walked along the shore quickly so as to reach my cabin before it was too late. It struck me how isolated it was out there. I had never felt like this before, and now I regretted that I had not arranged some other accommodation. By the time I shut the door behind me, the rain was already coursing down the windowpanes.

As one might imagine, there could be no question of sleep for me after all I had heard and experienced. I shut the door, drew the curtains closed across the windows and lit a lamp. I tried to read a book I had with me, but found myself scanning long passages over and over again without grasping what I was reading. I could not collect my thoughts. In the end, I set the book aside, shut my eyes and repeated to myself in a low voice the last sentence that Asbjørn Krag had said. 'Done for, aha. So that's what you think, is it?'

Little by little, I calmed down, dozed off, noticed the rain growing quieter before it finally ceased; in another minute or two I would have been quite asleep but was abruptly roused to wakefulness by the sound of a loud rapping.

Somebody was knocking at the door.

My first thought was: 'It's locked. A good thing too.' Another rap.

'Who is it?' I shouted.

No answer. My heart was pounding so hard I could count every beat. Of course, it was ridiculous of me to be afraid, but perhaps the fear came upon me so easily because I had just slipped out of a doze.

But then the knocking came again – hard, bony knuckles rapping on my door. It was an indescribable sensation, knowing that somebody was standing out there in the darkness. Who in the world could it be?

I asked again, called out as loudly as I could. After a long while came a reply, but I didn't catch it; the voice was low and muffled.

'Who is it?'

'Open up,' came the reply.

It was the detective. I drew back the bolt and flung the door open wide. There he stood, out in the dim light. He doffed his hat and gave an ironic bow, bending so low that his shining pate gleamed in the darkness.

'You?' I asked, astonished. 'Here so late?'

'Yes,' he replied. 'It is one o'clock. Did I frighten you?'

'Not at all.'

'Ah, come – just confess it. Were you asleep?'

'No.'

'Why aren't you in bed?'

I thought he was mocking me and became angry, but without waiting for my reply, the detective hurriedly said: 'I hope you will excuse me. But I come on an important errand.'

'Why didn't you answer the first time I asked you who you were?'

Asbjørn Krag laughed – silent, dry laughter. I could barely see the man so the laughter seemed to emanate from the dusk itself.

'Forgive me,' he replied. 'But I was conducting an experiment. I could tell that you were afraid and I thought it might be amusing to hear you one more time. That's it, I thought. That's the way a man cries out in fear.'

'You are mistaken,' I replied, and half-closed the door again. 'As well you may imagine, I am about to go to sleep. I do not wish to be disturbed.'

But without further ado the detective wedged his cane between the door and the threshold.

'Come with me,' he said. 'Why should you let me down just now?'

'What's going on? Has something happened?'

'Yes.'

Asbjørn Krag seemed so serious that I decided to go along with him after all. I put on my hat and then, as quietly as possible, opened the drawer in the table where I kept my revolver.

'Aha,' I heard the detective murmur. 'So you are arming yourself.'

'An old habit from my travels,' I answered. 'Besides, so many strange things are happening these days. Should I put on a raincoat?'

The detective looked up at the sky.

'The clouds are moving fast,' he said. 'We shall certainly not have any more rain.'

We left.

When we had walked a hundred paces or so, Asbjørn Krag stopped and said, 'You forgot to put out your lamp.'

He pointed towards my cabin, which now shone in the summer twilight like a real lighthouse.

'So I have,' I replied. 'But it doesn't matter. I'll be spared the trouble of lighting it again when I come back. This will not take long, I hope.'

The detective did not answer, but when we had walked another hundred paces, he asked, 'Did you forget to put out your lamp on purpose?'

'I don't understand you.'

Asbjørn Krag laughed again, a short, crackling laugh. 'Your cabin is in such a lonely spot,' he said. 'Terribly isolated. And this particular night is exceptionally dark.'

To soothe the outburst of anger that was seething in me, he took me companionably by the arm and apologised profusely for having disturbed me.

'Yes, and just why have you disturbed me?' I asked, impatiently.

'I shall tell you,' he replied. 'There are certain occasions when I do not trust my own senses. I have heard something tonight.'

'Have you been sitting up, then?'

'Yes, and not just tonight. I sleep very little, my dear fellow.'

'What did you hear?'

'I heard the iron chariot,' answered the detective.

He told his tale simply, with no drama, the way people will tell you about a piece of music they've heard, or a bird. We walked and walked, and the washing of the sea against the shore drowned out the sound of our footsteps.

'Perhaps you do not believe me,' continued the detective. 'You have not answered me.'

'Oh yes, I believe you. But what am I supposed to say?'

We opened a gate and walked past a few small houses. There was not a light to be seen and every window was dark; I felt as if the houses were empty and every human soul far, far away. We could not see a great deal: the road, the trees and the houses glided towards us out of the darkness as we walked, and we were encircled by a ring of black crags and rocky hilltops that stood etched against the sky like a palisade of darkness.

'Where are we going?' I asked.

'Out onto the plain,' Asbjørn Krag replied.

'Do you believe in the iron chariot?'

'I've heard it. I was standing by my open window and heard it in the distance, like a rattling of chains. The sound was borne to me on the gusts of wind. And now I want to go out onto the plain to see just what it is that is driving around out there at night.'

We walked into the forest, which closed about us oppressively; and now there was no sound any more either, for the whisper of the sea could not reach us up here. We quickened our pace.

'Do you think it will grow light soon?' I asked.

'Dawn will begin to break in half an hour,' Krag replied.

Even so, it was like emerging into twilight when we left the woods behind us – I could count the nearest tree trunks and see quite some way across the plain before the darkness obscured my sight. To our right, the rocky hilltop lifted a calm brow towards the flickering night sky. At the foot of the hill stood the sand-digger's hut, the broad overhang of its roof like an eyelid.

'Look at the grey hut,' said the detective. 'It is like an eye, staring at us sharply.'

Without thinking I added, pointlessly, 'Yes, but the body has been taken away now.'

We stood there for a while in silence, listening.

I didn't hear a thing.

'That damned watch,' whispered Asbjørn Krag. 'It's all I can hear.'

And then I became aware of the noise; I too heard its eternal tick-tock.

Krag snatched the watch from his pocket and stopped it.

But how such nights resonate with an incessant, deeply ringing note. If you do not listen, you sense only dead and total silence around you; but if you set your ear to this silence it begins at once to whisper. It may be the wind slipping gently through the treetops, which grows louder the longer you listen for it. But it need be nothing at all; it is as if the very silence whispers in your ear: drones and hums and grows into a fierce, distant storm; a hint, an impression of something vast and full of secrets that lies beyond all human senses.

But then comes a creak, a real sound – a footstep in the sand, a voice – and at once the silence returns. And then you find that you have heard nothing at all.

'Let us walk on,' said Krag.

I wanted to ask him where we were going. And I had got as far as saying, 'I don't quite understand where…' when Asbjørn Krag gripped my arm tightly.

There was no longer any need to strain our senses for now, loud and clear, far off in the distance, we could hear the distinctive ring of metal – like chains dragged along the ground by a column of slaves far beyond the horizon. It was the iron chariot.

The sound rose and fell. One moment it was so loud that we could actually hear the iron wheels thrumming on the axles, the next, it diminished again, glided far into the distance, clattered ten miles off, then subsided into silence, only to climb again and sing loudly in our ears.

We stood and listened to the iron chariot for ten minutes or more.

'I have a feeling that it is going in circles,' muttered Asbjørn Krag. 'That it is driving round in huge circles out there on the plain.'

He tried to bore through the darkness with his gaze, but could not. He cursed in irritation at the lack of light.

I asked whether we should run across the plain in the hope of catching a glimpse of this mysterious chariot.

'But which direction should we take?' asked Krag. 'It is impossible to tell where the sound is coming from. It is moving in great arcs – now to the north, now to the west. Listen, now it sounds as if it is coming closer.'

And it really did seem to be so, for the sound of clanking iron became more distinct and grew in strength.

A little later, Krag said, 'It cannot be far off now.'

'I can only hear the rattling of the wheels,' I whispered, 'but no horses' hooves. It must be a strange kind of chariot.'

But still we could not see it. The chariot worked its way into the darkness. Instinctively, we shrank towards the tree trunks, for we felt as if it might surge out of the darkness at any moment, charging past us all aglow.

Suddenly, Asbjørn Krag seized me by the arm.

'Did you hear that?' he whispered. His face was horribly tense.

'I can hear nothing but the iron chariot.'

'It seemed to me,' he murmured, 'that I heard a cry...but perhaps I am mistaken.'

Until then, the rolling of the chariot had come from straight ahead of us; but now it seemed to change direction and swing behind the woods. At once, the sound of iron was also muffled.

'Good God,' I cried. 'It is driving towards the sea.'

'Is there no road on that side of the woods?'

'No, no road – just rocky outcrops and sandy hollows.'

There was no longer any doubt about it. The chariot was driving straight for the sea, the sound of the rolling iron wheels becoming less distinct as it drew further and further into the distance.

'Surely it will be smashed to pieces,' I said. 'This is sheer madness.'

'And yet the sound is quite steady,' replied Asbjørn Krag, as he gazed over at the dark, jagged silhouette of the woods. 'It simply sounds further and further away.'

'It must soon reach the shore now,' I said, for I was familiar with the area. Krag nodded.

And then all at once the noise ceased.

'The chariot has stuck fast,' I cried.

'Or smashed to pieces,' answered Krag. 'Come, let us run over there.'

Without waiting to see what I would do, he set off at a dash. I followed, but he ran so fast and gained such a lead on me that he was on the point of vanishing ahead of me in the darkness.

We came to the other side of the forest and ran onwards down the slope. Now the darkness had yielded just enough for us to catch a glimpse of the sea below. The cold breath of the ocean rose to meet us; an icy chill pierced my breast. Krag stopped and looked across the huge slope. Here and there stood fir trees, their branches combed flat and twisted inland by the incessant sea breeze. The slope was full of boulders, of hollows, of sandbanks formed by the wind, whose wretched growth of wispy grass gave them a somewhat unshaven look. There was no road and it was almost impassable by foot, much less by vehicle. How could any carriage have driven here? It would instantly have been smashed to pieces. What's more, we had heard the regular, rhythmic rolling of its wheels, further and further off right up until the sound had stopped. What had become of it? We stared across the slope, our eyes darting around the breadth of it. But all we saw were tufts of grass and stones and sandbanks – and no sign of any chariot.

Asbjørn Krag walked a long way across the incline, his eyes fixed at all times on the ground.

When he turned back towards me, he said, 'No wheel tracks.'

'No wheel tracks?' I repeated, uncomprehendingly. 'So perhaps the chariot did not drive this way after all.'

'It cannot possibly have driven through the dense woodland,' said the detective. 'Come, let us go out onto the plain again.'

When we had walked so far that we could no longer see the ocean, Asbjørn Krag said: 'This is roughly where the chariot turned. That is how it seemed from the sound.'

'Or perhaps it was even further on,' I said.

Asbjørn Krag thought this over.

'Yes, perhaps,' he muttered.

We went a few steps further. Suddenly I stopped.

'Do you recognise this place?' I whispered.

The detective peered at me, almost maliciously.

'Yes,' he replied. 'I recognise it. Why have you gone so pale?'

'I have most certainly not gone pale,' I replied. 'Although perhaps all these sleepless nights have taken a toll on my nerves.'

I pointed. 'That spot over there is where we found the forestry inspector – over there by the grey stone; the dead man was lying there, face-down on the ground.'

Asbjørn Krag wrinkled his forehead.

'The grey stone, absolutely not,' he murmured. He looked around intently. 'I cannot understand where that stone came from.'

I laughed and replied, 'And yet the stone is there. It is lying in exactly the same place where we found the dead man.'

Asbjørn Krag went over to the spot. I watched him bend down over the grey stone. A quick dash, and I was there too.

It was not a grey stone at all, but a person lying there – an old man. He had a hideous wound on the back of his head.

'He's dead,' said Asbjørn Krag, turning him over so that we could see his face. 'He died less than a quarter of an hour ago.'

I no longer remember what I thought or felt at that moment. I was probably not thinking clearly. I looked at the dead man uncomprehendingly, with a paralysing sense of being in some mysterious, unreal existence. And I was quite speechless. But I do recall that I behaved in a mindless and confused fashion. I bent down and fingered the dead man's clothing: striped, a thick plain weave. Asbjørn Krag roused me by saying, 'The iron chariot has killed him.'

'The iron chariot,' I muttered.

'Yes,' replied the detective. 'Don't you recognise him?'

I looked at the old grey face. Yes, but where had I seen him before? Unwittingly, my thoughts brushed past a memory.

'Don't you remember that portrait?' the detective asked sharply. 'The portrait in Gjærnæs's parlour? That goatee beard, that crooked nose, those small eye-sockets?'

I looked at the detective in horror.

'Of course, of course,' I stammered. 'Old Gjærnæs. It's old Gjærnæs lying there. But good God – he drowned four years ago!'

'Nonetheless. Only now is he dead,' replied Asbjørn Krag.

The detective took me gently by the arm.

'You are unsteady,' he said. 'There's no doubt about it: this has taken a toll on your nerves.'

Now my lips were growing cold again, and I felt the warm whisper on my neck and the back of my head that has always warned me of a fainting fit. I looked about me. The landscape took on the most extraordinary aspect in my confused eyes. I saw the daylight dawning. A long arm of light reached out across the plain and plucked at the forest, turning the trunks of the outermost firs golden. I looked at the dead man, at Asbjørn Krag, and then let my gaze wander over the plain. I understood nothing and for a few seconds I was overwhelmed by the distinct feeling of being in a dream; yet my senses were alive and receptive, and a strange image of the sunrise, seen for a tenth of a second, burnt itself upon my consciousness. The sky to the east was no longer sky, but an abyss of light leading into remote and undreamt-of worlds; a rampart of clouds exploded from the horizon and these clouds were transformed into a fantastical parade of astonishing beasts with fiery manes, embers sparking beneath their winged hooves; a tumbling horde harnessed by the reins of the sun's twinkling beams – the golden draught horses of the day. And then the sun itself rolled thunderously up from the horizon.

From far, far away, I heard Asbjørn Krag's voice.

V

The Face

I WAS UNCONSCIOUS FOR SEVERAL HOURS. I came around when I felt somebody giving me a vigorous shake. I was lying on a wagon. I heard a voice and saw a familiar face. It was the police chief.

'Ah, so you've come to now,' he said. 'Just lie there and stay calm. We shall soon be there.'

'What time is it?' I asked.

'Seven,' he replied.

'Seven in the morning?'

He laughed.

'Yes,' he answered.

The night's adventure was still unclear to me. I dared not ask. I did not know whether I had been dreaming or whether I had been ill.

'Where is Asbjørn Krag?'

The police chief answered, with a jerk of the head, 'Out there.

Out on the plain.'

So it must have happened after all. I raised myself up in the wagon. We were already down by the harbour where people were tending to their boats; soon I could be in my cabin. A terrible fatigue had come over me and I yearned for a bed, for a long, long rest.

It disgusted me to be so weak, and so I descended stiffly from the carriage unaided. When I entered my cabin, I saw that the lamp was still burning on the table. I put it out and hurled myself straight into bed. When I awoke at four o'clock in the afternoon, Asbjørn Krag was sitting in my room.

I felt completely refreshed and wanted to get up.

'Lie there for a little while longer,' said Asbjørn Krag. 'It will do you the world of good to have a rest.'

'I have had a most peculiar night,' I replied. 'I do not know what I dreamt and what I actually experienced.'

The detective smiled.

'We did not, at any rate, chase down the iron chariot,' he said. 'And that was what we were after.'

'No, I remember that. We didn't find any tracks either.'

'It does not leave any tracks.'

'Are you trying to make me believe in that ghostly chariot, my dear Krag?'

'Not in the least. But the iron chariot leaves no tracks.'

'Have you perhaps discovered the secret?'

'Yes.'

'And found the chariot?'

'No, but it will not be long before I find it. Once you are quite well again, we shall go out on another expedition together and then we shall find the iron chariot.'

'Another expedition,' I murmured, looking at the detective uncertainly, enquiringly.

He smiled again.

'I can guess your thoughts,' he said. 'You are afraid to ask.'

And I truly was. I was afraid to ask. In my mind's eye I could still so clearly see the dead man out on the plain, old Gjærnæs who had drowned four years before. I must have been dreaming, of course, but dreaming with the most terrible clarity and vividness; that whole sunrise still vibrated in my consciousness, I could recall every detail – the tufts of grass out on the plain, the tree trunks, the gleam as of silver in the first light of day, and then the dead man's clothing made of coarse striped material. But that must have been a dream, of course.

'I have to leave this place,' I said. 'I am becoming afraid of these shocks.'

'Yes, you're not as strong as I first thought,' replied the detective. 'This most recent experience has hit you pretty hard. If I had not caught you in my arms, you would have fallen straight to the ground.'

I raised myself up in my bed. Ah, now I could still feel it, that clammy whisper in my brain.

'Be frank with me,' I urged him. 'Tell me what happened to us last night.'

'Surely you must remember it quite as well as I do.'

I had no wish to go directly into the matter, so I asked instead, 'Have you spoken to young Gjærnæs?'

'Yes,' replied the detective. 'He has just driven home.'

'Alone or with company?'

'No living company.' The detective got up from the chair and paced back and forth across the room, deep in thought.

'My dear Krag,' I continued. 'Are you trying to tell me that we really did experience all the things I think I experienced?'

The detective stopped in front of me and looked at me for a long time in silence.

90

'Yes,' he replied. 'We had some remarkable experiences last night.'

'It seems to me that we found a dead man.'

'Yes.'

'An old man. And we found him on precisely the same spot where we found the murdered forestry inspector, Blinde, three weeks ago.'

Asbjørn Krag nodded.

'Precisely the same spot where we thought the iron chariot had turned to go down towards the sea.'

He nodded again.

'But the old man,' I stammered. 'The old man… It's impossible of course, though, my dear Krag… It cannot be possible.'

'The old man,' Krag continued my sentence calmly, 'was the father of young Gjærnæs.'

'But he drowned four years ago, didn't he?'

'No, he cannot have done so.'

'Can't he…?'

'That much is obvious, after all,' answered the detective. 'For he was alive until at least two o'clock this morning.'

'But his boat drifted ashore, capsized, out among the skerries,' I murmured.

'And his hat was washed up too,' continued the detective, as he walked over to the window and pushed the blind aside. 'All the props were in place.'

I gave this some thought. I began to suspect where the detective was heading.

'So you think,' I asked, 'that old Gjærnæs staged the whole drowning?'

'Yes.'

'That he fled, vanished – and purposely allowed people to believe he had drowned.'

'Yes.'

'But why – why?'

Asbjørn Krag took up his station at my bedside once more.

'I shall tell you,' he said. 'Old Gjærnæs was a swindler. Only death has saved him from being charged with insurance fraud.'

'How do you know?'

'I have long had my suspicions, but now at last they have been fully confirmed – in part through seeing the old man and in part from hearing young Gjærnæs's account. My dear fellow, you have been labouring under the illusion that I was living the life of a holidaying gentleman out here – spending all my time on walks, reading, eating and bathing. And yet every single minute of every day and night when I have not been asleep I have been concerned solely with this terrible affair. I have gone for walks, it is true, but I have always done so with a purpose connected to the case – whether because there was something I needed to look at or somebody I needed to speak to. At mealtimes, I have assiduously engaged in conversations and on many occasions I have led the discussion where I would have it go. And when I have apparently been busy reading, I have in fact been spending hour after hour in solitude, meditating or comparing and turning to account the reports I have received from my agents.'

'Your agents?' I asked. 'But you have been operating quite alone all the time you have been down here.'

'Down here, yes,' the detective replied. 'Here at the focal point of events, I have been quite alone. But I have had my agents in Kristiania and elsewhere. Detectives need a great deal of information and I have received a great deal of information about both Gjærnæs and the murdered forestry inspector.'

'But surely you could obtain better information here on the spot,' I objected.

'Far from it,' the detective replied. 'I did not wish to have information only about the forestry inspector's life just prior to his death. I also wanted to know what he was in the habit of doing in his ordinary, everyday life. He came from Kristiania, after all.'

'I have met him in Kristiania myself.'

'I know,' said the detective. 'I have also received reports about the people he used to mix with. You were not among his closest companions, but you did meet him now and then at parties – for the most part those to which Hilde Gjærnæs was also invited.'

'I do not recall it so precisely, but that may well be the case. Hilde Gjærnæs and I moved in the same circles while she was living in Kristiania and the forestry inspector was in love with Hilde, after all. Naturally he took the trouble to go to the places where she would be.'

'A most logical deduction,' the detective replied, the ironic smile flitting across his face once more. 'Very well. But we shall not talk so much about the forestry inspector just now. We shall talk about old Gjærnæs.'

'Of course. So what have you learned about him?'

'One of the first things I discovered was that he had taken out a life insurance policy for 30,000 kroner. You know yourself that when he vanished four years ago – or drowned, as people thought – his affairs were in exceedingly bad shape. His son later established some kind of order in the business, essentially thanks to the 30,000 kroner paid out by the insurance company. Young Gjærnæs told me that, unfortunately, his father had left two false bills of exchange behind him. And these bills were hanging over the old man's head at precisely that time, four years ago; it was fear of a catastrophe that drove him to act out his bold and terrible comedy. Old Gjærnæs was passionately keen on fishing, so there was nothing remotely surprising about his leaving the farm alone to go on a fishing trip at three in the morning on 24th August. Later in the day, his capsized boat was found and his hat drifted ashore. I have reason to believe that he planned his flight most shrewdly. He had taken with him all the available cash, a couple of thousand kroner. Several days ago, I investigated the steamship routes from that time and it seems that on just that day, 24th August, a steamship left here for Kristiania at seven in the morning. He probably disguised himself and, after arriving in Kristiania, travelled abroad. So he will have read news of his own death in the papers.'

'A peculiar tale,' I muttered in horror. 'Can this really have happened?'

'Yes,' the detective replied. 'And you are quite wrong if you think there is anything unique about it. On the contrary – this type of insurance fraud is well documented, especially in international criminology. My legal library contains an interesting example of a man over in England who managed to die fourteen times before he was eventually caught, alive and well.'

'I have a feeling,' I said, 'that you had your suspicions about this the whole time.'

'I had a certain suspicion that something of this nature was afoot,' corrected the detective. 'But I certainly did not think that we were dealing with such a clear-cut case of fraud. By the time I arrived here, I already had a good deal of information, more than you could suspect. I knew the story of old Gjærnæs's unfortunate death, I knew about his false bills of exchange, and I knew about the insurance payment that was disbursed to his son immediately after his death, returning the family affairs to order. You must concede that I already had most excellent material; to use detective jargon, I had an abundance of suspicious circumstances at my fingertips. I established that old Gjærnæs had left the stage at a remarkably convenient moment; and precisely because this case greatly reminded me of another similar affair that had recently occurred in Holland, my suspicions were roused – although, to be sure, I was unable to find any connection whatsoever between the murder of the forestry inspector and the death of old Gjærnæs.'

As the detective continued his account I listened with growing excitement. Asbjørn Krag spoke slowly and concisely, as if he were thinking each sentence through before he uttered it. His account sounded remarkably like an expert summing-up.

'But then I came down here,' he said. 'And when I heard about your experiences on the night of the forestry inspector's murder, I advanced another step. You were refused entry to the house – and in a most ostentatious manner to boot. I realised that there must be something inside, within the walls, that you were not meant to see.'

'But the forestry inspector,' I objected.

'Yes, the forestry inspector,' replied Asbjørn Krag. 'He occupied a special position. The forestry inspector was about to become a member of the family; it was necessary to acquaint him with the terrible secret. So I understood something had happened that evening, something very serious. The same night that the forestry inspector was killed out on the plain.'

'Yes, but how will you get it all to tally?' I asked. 'Why should the poor fellow be killed?'

'How would you explain it?'

'Perhaps young Gjærnæs regretted telling him. Perhaps the forestry inspector withdrew from the engagement and threatened to report the secret to the police. And so he drove after him…and then he…'

'Do you believe that?' asked the detective.

And it struck me that Asbjørn Krag was smiling again, with an air of teasing malice. But then at once he became serious and said, 'From the very first instant I have been quite aware that there was no connection. I do not believe young Gjærnæs is the murderer.'

'So who is, then?'

Instead of replying the detective asked, 'Shall I continue?'

'Yes, please. Do go on,' I said, leaning back in my bed, my arms folded behind my neck. I listened intently as the detective continued.

'My investigations in the neighbourhood further confirmed me in my suspicion that something extraordinary had happened at the farm that night, something significant and serious. Even before visiting the farm, I had learnt of the owner's disturbed behaviour. And as soon as I set eyes on the steward and had an opportunity to speak to the young master, I was absolutely certain that some secret was being concealed. Although the story of the father's drowning had not come to the forefront in my chain of reasoning, my thoughts constantly touched upon it; I could not get it to fit in, though I tried over and over again. In the game I was playing, the father's death was an important move, or more precisely, it was an important piece, but I simply had no idea where to place it in order to make the whole game work out once and for all. You will remember that I was interested in the portrait of the old man that was hanging in Gjærnæs's study. Very well, but do you remember the door...?'

'The door?' I said. 'What do you mean?'

'My dear fellow,' continued Asbjørn Krag. 'The small matter of the closed door was one of the most important aspects of our visit to Gjærnæs Farm. Do you pay no attention to what does and doesn't happen? If I observe the events around me attentively, I know that this or that will happen if all is well.

But if things do not go as I had expected, I know there is some definite reason for it, which I must try and discover. In this way I have often been led to the very heart of a great many secrets. Don't you find it odd that Miss Hilde was not present during our visit?'

'There was good reason for it,' I replied. 'She was sick and overwhelmed by events. Her brother explicitly told us that she had gone to bed.'

'That is quite right. And therefore I also asked to inspect the interior of the farm.'

'Therefore?'

'Quite so. Because I concluded on the spot that if Miss Hilde was in bed, we would naturally be unable to see her apartment. But that was just what we did do: we were able to see right into her pale blue bedroom. She was not there.'

'She was elsewhere,' I answered. 'She was in the room next to the library.'

'Indeed, she was behind the door. I do believe she was actually there. But now I must ask you to recall one thing. When we were in the library, I made an attempt to go through that closed door. But Gjærnæs immediately barred my way. The mere thought that I might slip in there appeared to terrify him. At that moment I became absolutely convinced that he was concealing something. You can probably guess who was in the room beside the library?'

'Miss Hilde,' I replied.

'Highly likely – but somebody else was with her. And that somebody else was Gjærnæs's father, the old man whom we found dead out on the plain last night.'

I lay in bed, nerves aquiver as I listened to the detective's account. I had long understood where he was heading and slowly I glided into the sure conviction that everything I recalled of the night's events was real and not a dream. I wanted him to say it himself…and yet a great shudder ran through me when I heard him remark, in his dry, resonant voice: 'The old man whom we found dead out on the plain last night.'

The detective added, smiling once more, 'So, my dear fellow, you did not dream it.'

'You read my mind,' I murmured.

Asbjørn Krag sat in silence for almost a minute, a silence I found oppressive. I became increasingly nervous, and wished the detective far away so that I could get up and go out into the free, fresh air I could hear whispering about the house.

I peered up at Asbjørn Krag. He sat between the window and the bed, his chiselled profile, his bald pate and his broad jaw etched sharply against the light. Why didn't he speak? What was he thinking about? Suddenly, he turned his face towards me and I could see that his eyes were shining, unnaturally enlarged by the glass of his pince-nez.

'Yes,' he said. 'I can read you like an open book.'

'Who killed him?' I whispered rapidly.

'Which of the two?'

'The old man – the father – whom we found last night.'

'Shall I go on?' asked Krag.

'Of course,' I replied, as I let my gaze wander to another part of the room. 'Do go on.'

And so the detective continued. 'When I left Gjærnæs Farm, I noticed the comedy between the owner and the steward, of course, but feigned not to have observed it, because I knew the steward was my man. Sooner or later, that man must come to me and tell me what he knew. And it was clear to me at once that he knew something. He was weighed down by his knowledge; bad conscience shone from his eyes. I am staying at the hotel, I said. That was enough. And so he came, a few days later, and told all. And in the meantime, I had obtained fresh information. After hearing the steward's tale, I became convinced that Gjærnæs was hiding his father at the farm. After all, this fact would entirely explain his nervousness and peculiar behaviour. As for the steward, he apparently remains under the illusion that Gjærnæs has something to do with the murder of Forestry Inspector Blinde. And it was a strange chance that he should have received the letter from his father on exactly the same night as the crime was committed. After Blinde had left the farm, Gjærnæs drove across the island to meet the old man, who had arrived at one of the mail boat stops in utmost secrecy. That is why he had to drive out, quietly and alone; but he mismanaged things: he should have taken his steward entirely into his confidence – had he done so, we might never have shone a light on this terrible drama.'

The detective stopped again and slowly – so slowly it seemed almost like affectation – he drew a cigar case from his pocket. He selected a cigar, lit it, puffed some thick, white clouds of smoke into the air and then sat with the case in his hand.

'This is made of quite ordinary leather,' he said. 'But it has a silver trim. Blinde's missing cigar case was made of green alligator skin, was it not?'

'It definitely wasn't a cigar case,' I replied. 'It was a wallet.'

Asbjørn Krag blew a great smoke ring into the air then began to laugh.

'Of course,' he answered. 'But didn't it have a gold trim?'

'I don't know… I never heard anything about that.'

The detective turned to face me. He was still laughing.

'I want to get up,' I said. 'I still feel a little weak. I'd like to go out in the fresh air.'

At that, Asbjørn Krag held up an admonishing hand.

'Under no circumstances,' he replied, gravely. 'First, I must finish my tale. I am averse to lengthy interruptions… Besides, I can open the windows.'

'Yes, thank you – do open the windows. All the windows.'

'But my dear fellow,' he said. 'The windows are already open, they have been open the whole time.'

He laughed. I said no more and dared not look at him. I was afraid I might flare up into a terrible outburst of rage. I listened as he snapped the cigar case closed and put it in his pocket.

'How well I can understand it,' he murmured in a low voice shortly afterwards, as if he were talking to himself. 'How well I understand Gjærnæs's behaviour at this time. He wasn't frightened about the murder. When he spoke about the killing of the forestry inspector, he did so absent-mindedly, almost indifferently. He had other, more serious matters on his mind; it didn't even occur to him that he might fall under suspicion. On the other hand, the secret of his father lay upon him like a dreadful weight; the catastrophe had come so suddenly, was so absolutely harrowing, that it made him distracted and foolish. For he must, at all costs, hide the farm's mysterious third inhabitant. And he was so eager, so haphazard in his efforts to protect the secret that he quite failed to notice that he was exposing himself to suspicion. In the end, anybody at all could point to him and say: he killed the forestry inspector. He positively gave himself away as the murderer. But only thoughtless people think that way; fools without the slightest spark of deductive power. It was clear to me with even half an eye that it was impossible for the man who had committed the crime out on the plain to behave in this way. Even the stupidest individual would not go about giving himself away like this, little by little. No, he had a great secret to protect: the murder was no concern of his, so he had no time to think about it. Then yesterday, the steward went to him and said: "I'm going to see the detective and tell him everything. For my conscience's sake, I cannot remain silent any longer." The steward still believed there was a connection with the murder. But young Gjærnæs simply could not conceive of the possibility that he meant anything other than the secret of the old man risen from the dead. So what could Gjærnæs have said to the steward other than what he did say: "What business is it of the detective's? It is a private matter." I sent the steward back to his master with a message that you may have found odd. I asked him to tell me a time when I could come to visit him. I did not want to arrive without forewarning as I had no wish to risk a new catastrophe – I knew I could expect anything of Gjærnæs in his current state of mind. And there was also another particular intention behind my behaviour: it was a way of forcing Gjærnæs to send his father away from the farm. He would not dare keep him there any longer if he was expecting a visit from me. I guessed that he would send him away from the farm that very night. And I was right. However, my dear fellow, in this way I also became inadvertently complicit in the old man's death.'

'You!' I cried. 'Did you kill him?'

The detective shook his head.

'As I already told you,' he replied, 'the iron chariot killed him – that strange and calamitous vehicle that rolls and rolls along without leaving any tracks behind it. I knew that the old man would come across the plain, that he must pass by this spot to reach the steamer. And I kept watch on the road, having determined that I would go up to him, lay a hand on his shoulder and say: "My dear fellow, let us have a little chat." But while I was wandering about awaiting his arrival, I heard the iron chariot.'

The detective concluded, 'That is the story, all that I can tell you. The rest you already know.'

'I am none the wiser,' I replied, 'absolutely none the wiser than when you began. You say the iron chariot killed old Gjærnæs. But what is this iron chariot – where does it come from and who is driving it?'

'I have asked myself that very question time and time again,' replied the detective. 'And I did not find the answer until last night.'

'So you know the secret of the iron chariot, then?'

'Yes.'

Asbjørn Krag looked at his watch.

'It is now half-past five,' he said. 'In an hour, the tide will be out, and we may catch a glimpse of the iron chariot.'

'The tide?' I asked, astonished.

'Yes,' replied Krag. 'The iron chariot is no more. It has drowned.'

The detective spoke gravely and there was nothing remotely playful about his manner.

'When we find the iron chariot,' he said, 'you will understand a great deal about what now seems mysterious and obscure to you. I am beginning to believe that this case has been as simple as can be from the outset. But by a curious trick of fate, the original case became entangled with a number of mysterious circumstances that came into play at the same time yet actually have nothing to do with it. This has happened before over the course of my professional life. You cannot imagine how impossible it can make an investigation when two cases that have no connection to one another get mixed up. Now first and foremost in this case, we have young Gjærnæs's compromising behaviour, which points directly towards his involvement in the death of the forestry inspector; next the murder, and then the iron chariot, which also seems to be a part of it. As long as I based my deductions on the assumption that these three phenomena were connected, all I could see was confusion and still more confusion. But as soon as I began to separate them, to disentangle the threads of the mystery, it all became much clearer. My dear fellow, we are not dealing with just one case but three. First, young and old Gjærnæs, that is a case in itself; then the iron chariot, a case in itself.'

'And then the murders,' I said.

'The murder,' corrected the detective. 'There was only one. Old Gjærnæs was not murdered. Only the forestry inspector.'

'But have you no idea who killed the forestry inspector, then?' I asked.

'Oh yes,' Asbjørn Krag replied. 'I could go and point him out this very day.'

The detective walked quickly out of my room. He called in to me, 'I shall sit out here and wait for you. But you must hurry now: ebb-tide is at six o'clock.'

'So do you promise me that I shall get to see the iron chariot?' I asked excitedly.

'I shall do what I can,' he replied.

'I believe you can achieve what no other man is capable of,' I called out to him. 'You are a veritable wizard.'

'I am only human,' replied Asbjørn Krag. 'But I am seldom wrong. Do hurry now.'

I got dressed quickly. There was fever in my blood. Was it from the suspense of the detective's tale or was it a reaction triggered by my fainting fit? It was almost certainly both the one and the other, but I knew at least that I was very much looking forward to being in the open air. Asbjørn Krag's endless, unravelling talk about the dead old man, about the murder, about the iron chariot had gradually had a thoroughly depressing effect on me. What's more, my room smelt of camphor, while the sea outside filled my window with bright blue.

At last I was ready. Asbjørn Krag sat waiting on a stone by the edge of the road.

As things turned out, I did not get to see the iron chariot after all, and nor was the secret surrounding this ominous vehicle revealed. Still, it was something of a consolation to me that Asbjørn Krag was probably just as disappointed as I.

The detective drew me with him across the plain to the place where we had heard the iron chariot roll down towards the sea the night before. It had fallen quite still and several small boats lay just offshore, while the people in them searched in the sea with long poles and plumb lines.

'Searching for the iron chariot?' I asked.

Asbjørn Krag nodded.

'It drove into the sea here.'

Asbjørn Krag directed the search efforts for an hour. Little by little he became impatient, because nobody found anything whatsoever. And then the water began to rise. And the detective was obliged to call a halt to the work for that day.

'A bad business,' he muttered in irritation. 'I shall have to wire Kristiania.'

He wrote a telegram and sent the message to the telegraph office.

And then we wended our way back to the hotel. Dusk was already beginning to fall.

Asbjørn Krag, who had been so tremendously talkative through the whole afternoon, remarkably so, had now become tight-lipped. Still, I did learn that old Gjærnæs's body had been taken to the farm and that the son would travel to the capital the very next day to settle matters with the insurance company.

As we stood on the hotel veranda, which was teeming with guests, I whispered in Asbjørn Krag's ear: 'Won't you point out the criminal?'

But the detective just shook his head.

'Not yet,' he said.

He truly was a peculiar man. At times, he could erupt into bursts of outright garrulousness, but then, with no apparent cause, become abruptly taciturn and reserved. I had the distinct impression that the latter state was, in fact, the one that came most naturally to him and that he became loquacious only because he had some – to me, inexplicable – intention.

But whether he spoke or was silent, he always had that mocking twitch about his mouth, and his eyes were always attentive, scrutinising.

He could come up with the most peculiar questions, surprising and apparently quite meaningless. Like this evening. It was already half-past ten and I was sitting in conversation with some of my friends among the guests. I felt no desire to retire for the night and when somebody proposed a hand of cards, I was keen to play. I was on my way into one of the rooms to fetch the cards and when I pushed the door open, I found myself suddenly face to face with Asbjørn Krag, whom I had not seen for the past hour or so. I gave a start; one does tend to give an involuntary jump when one finds a person in a room one had believed to be empty.

'I thought you had gone back to your cabin,' he said.

'As you see,' I replied. 'I have not left. I shall sit here for a while yet.'

Asbjørn Krag twisted his face into a grimace. His great white teeth positively shone in the darkness.

'You probably don't much like that lonely cabin of yours,' he said.

I could find no reply to this. I was simply astonished; it was not the first time the detective had spoken almost menacingly about the isolated location of my little cabin.

Asbjørn Krag seized me by the jacket collar and continued, 'Listen. There is something I wish to ask you. You have just one window in your room, do you not?'

'Yes, but it is very large. Why do you ask?'

'Is the window not equipped with a blind?'

'Why, yes.'

'Do you generally roll this blind down at night?'

I laughed.

'I don't understand this joke of yours,' I said.

'I am not joking.'

'Very well, since the matter is of such interest to you, I am pleased to inform you that when the sun is out, I keep the blind rolled down.'

'But at night?' he asked. 'When your lamp is lit. What then?'

'What does it matter? I have no neighbours and my cabin looks straight out to sea. I do not always roll my blind down just because I have lit my lamp.'

Asbjørn Krag grinned again with his white teeth.

'But if the window is not covered,' he said, 'it is as if the room is open to the darkness. Somebody could be outside looking in.'

The detective loosened his grip on my jacket collar. I backed away from him a pace.

'You really are making the most peculiar efforts to frighten me,' I said. 'Do you take me for a child? I am not afraid of the dark.'

'Forgive me,' he replied meekly. 'It was not my intention to startle you. But when I start pondering something, I find myself asking the oddest questions from sheer thoughtlessness. By the way, you might do me a favour.'

'Now, tonight?' I asked, in a disapproving tone, shaking the deck of cards to draw his attention to the fact that I had other things to do.

'I'm writing a report at the moment,' he said, 'and I have reached the description of the body.'

I shuddered, and all at once a sinister air swept through the semi-dark room where we two stood alone.

'The body?' I stammered. 'You are writing about the body?'

'Naturally. I must make a report, after all. Now, what did the body look like? Think about it.'

'Dark brown hair,' I began, without thinking.

Asbjørn Krag clapped me lightly on the shoulder.

'My dear fellow,' he said. 'Why didn't you ask which body I meant? But yes, you are right, I am writing about the dead forestry inspector at present. Now would you be so kind as to listen and see if I have got anything wrong: his dark brown hair was combed with a clear parting on the left-hand side. He had somewhat large, protruding ears, his forehead was high and very pale, in contrast to the lower part of his face, which was tanned by sun and wind. The striking pallor of his brow was due to the fact that he always went about with his hat pulled down over his eyes. His beard was silky soft and reddish, very well-tended and slightly curled; his lips, which were not hidden by his beard, were well-formed, red and plump with blood. His eyes were almost light blue, but since his irises were very small and his eyeballs large, the whites formed a kind of belt around the irises, giving him a staring expression. His beard grew a long way down his neck, which was short and thick. When he was found, his stiff shirt collar was snapped in several places, and his green tie had been pushed up towards his right ear. That is what the murdered man looked like, is it not?'

'Yes,' I answered. 'As far as I can tell, your description is very accurate.'

'Yes, thank you. That was all I wanted to know,' said Asbjørn Krag, staring straight ahead in a most peculiar fashion. There was something piercing and unpleasant about his look. I opened the door so that the light fell upon him. The detective was pale but smiling. He nodded to me and smiled. Ah, that eternal smile.

I went quickly out into the lounge. My friends were sitting waiting. I set down the cards and said, 'You must find another fourth, gentlemen. I shall not be playing with you.'

All at once I had lost any inclination to play. I sat and listened out for the sound of the detective's footsteps as they disappeared through the rooms. Protruding, slightly large ears, a high pale forehead, red lips that were not hidden by his beard. Wherever I turned my eyes, I seemed to see the dead man's features… The collar was snapped…the green tie was pushed up towards the right ear… To distract my attention from this frightful image, I interfered with the other guests' game in a most impolite fashion, pointing out errors where there were none whatsoever, and loudly expressing approbation for no reason. My actions provoked much disapproval and many enraged glances. In the end, I left.

I walked past Asbjørn Krag's window. There was light within and the blind was rolled down but I saw no shadow; I dare say he was sitting calmly at his desk writing about the dead man's appearance in his report.

The evening was overcast and hazy, and there was no longer any wind at all. But the rain and bluster of the previous night had brought the cold along with them. The strange thing about the high summer is that although the land is laden with growth and everything is ripe and ready to fall, too heavy now for the stems to bear, and although the earth exudes the warm scent of abundance, a cold day can still come for no reason whatsoever, freezing the potato leaves; it is a waft of autumn, it is October's icy fingers plucking from afar – but it only lasts for a few hours before the heat reasserts its oppressive supremacy.

And this was just such an evening, with a hint of autumn in the air, a breath of cold upon my knuckles. The darkness tried to settle in beneath the cloudy sky, but did not quite succeed, for the yellow wheat fields, the red houses and the grey dust of the road still contrived to feebly assert their colours.

But the unseasonable sadness of the evening affected my mood; a strange listlessness came over me, accompanied by a great longing to be far, far away – in cities with narrow streets and crowds of people. I thought to myself: this sinister murder case is getting a grip on you. You must leave…

Now I was on the road to my lonely cabin. As I came down towards the sea, I saw by my watch that it was already past midnight. I stopped close to the jetty; from here, I could see my cabin out at the end of the headland, like a white gravestone in the darkness. And I suddenly had an urge to wait a while longer before walking home. I wasn't actually afraid of anything, but I had a feeling that I would have a great deal of trouble lighting my lamp. I drifted down to the jetty. There was nobody there and I did not see a single living soul in the vicinity, either – people had gone home. And all the houses looked dead and abandoned, the way houses always look at night when there are no lights shining in the windows or people moving around outside.

The seaweed stood up straight in the water, motionless. I could hear a faint grinding down on the seashore, and now and then the sea sobbed against the dark piles of the jetty, with a sound like smashing china; the small boats lay moored on slack ropes, bobbing against one another like corks in a puddle, and further out lay a great open sloop, brim-full of darkness. For the gloom was not powerful enough to cover everything: it gathered in nooks and crannies, in corners, under jetties and it filled the woods; but it could not conquer the rocky hilltops, which lifted up their bright foreheads, nor the rounded skerries that framed the open sea, where a lead-grey strip of ocean shone.

I stared out over the edge of the jetty for a long time, counting the jellyfish that floated in the sea like drops of blood. I waited to see if I would hear a human voice. But it was as if all men were dead: I heard no oars slapping, no cries, no noise. I left the jetty and set off along the road to the cabin. I walked quickly.

The road lay like a narrow ribbon between the sea and a sheer rock face, so nobody could pass by me unseen. But I did not expect to meet anybody either, for I lived alone in the cabin and who would think of visiting me so late? I walked onwards to the cabin, whose doorway faced me, while the window on the other side looked out to sea.

A strange thought seized me. It was certainly a presentiment of what was to come. I thought: what if there is a person sitting waiting for me inside the cabin? There was a rickety old rocking chair in my room and I could not rid myself of the thought that perhaps a person was sitting in the chair – I even had an idea of this person's appearance, a chalk-white brow… When I walked in, the person would be sitting quite calmly in the rocking chair, white brow shining in the darkness, and would say not a word… I walked more and more quickly, hastened to arrive lest this peculiar fear, which grew and grew, should entirely overpower me. Before I quite knew it, I was standing in the middle of my room. The rocking chair was empty. I closed the door behind me.

As I fumbled around for the matches, I distinctly heard the ticking of a watch – but it was not mine. I felt an icy terror grip my heart and came close to walking out of the door again, but then I remembered the death-watch beetle, the little insect that sings in old houses. It was just the death-watch beetle I could hear – and I continued to search for the matches. But I couldn't help listening out for the intense ticking, which seemed to move around, to follow me; and in my confused imagination, I thought that some person was following me with noiseless tread, a person I could not see but whose watch I could hear. At last I found the matches and took the glass cover off the lamp. It was warm. The glass cover of the lamp was warm.

I stood as if paralysed, the glass in one hand and a burning match in the other. The match burnt down until its flame singed my fingers and then it went out, and everything was in darkness. But the only feeling that struck me then was a great longing to scatter the darkness, to cast light around me. I do not remember how it happened, but all at once I found I had managed to light the lamp, and my eyes involuntarily sought out the window. It was a big, old-fashioned window, divided into eight smaller panes. The darkness stood pressed up against these eight panes, making them black as ebony. The blind! I leapt up to close it, trembling with fear.

But then I saw it, out in the darkness – a face looking in at me. It was the murdered man…that high forehead, the pink lips that separated his beard and moustache like an open wound… the face was clearly framed in the ebony-black darkness. The face came closer. Now I could also see the neck, the snapped collar and the tie that was twisted up towards the right ear. The dead man was about to climb into the room.

VI

The Dog

I STAGGERED AWAY FROM THE WINDOW, turned my face to the wall and knelt there for several minutes, leaning against the side of the bed. In a voice that sounded strange and distant, I cried out several times in breathless fear: 'No, no, no!'

I dared not turn my eyes towards the window, not for the world; but I could feel it on the back of my neck, how that frightful face out in the darkness drew closer. Now, it was floating in through the green panes of glass, gliding through the glass like a body hauled through the sea – slow and dreadful, silent and stealing ever closer. I dared not look over there, not for the world, but suddenly I turned my head.

There it was again, the face, white and gruesome, with its high forehead, lips pink as a child's. I hurled myself upon the bed and hid my eyes, but felt a breath of icy terror on my neck, a chill as if from the corpse-light of the moon.

When I came around from a fainting fit that must have lasted an hour, the grey light of dawn was seeping into the room. I still could not bring myself to look towards the window, but knew that it was becoming steadily lighter outside. I felt as if I were lying in a little cabin on board a ship that had journeyed through the darkness, and now the day and the light were coming nearer.

But as I began to see the objects around me more clearly, my fear slipped away. And when I saw the charming old parlour clock, stopped for a generation, the small oil prints, the picture of Norway's Founding Fathers of 1905, the vases and the white papers on the table – all of it homely and free of peril – it rapidly became clear to me that, all things considered, I had behaved in a quite undignified fashion. This was the second time I had fainted; I was weaker than a hysterical woman. I looked over at the window.

Outside, the trees stood motionless against a sodden grey sky. I opened the window and the curtains filled at once like billowing sails although there was no wind. But the air itself was heavy and oppressive – it was filled with ocean bluster, tinged blue with the bright reflections of the summer waves, and bore with it a delightful breath of high summer, which wafted from great, newly threshed hayfields, from wind-dried, sun-drenched cloudberry heaths, from the spruce forests, carrying with it their aroma of resin and rotting fir-cones, and it had surely wandered about many a secretive boulder-strewn slope, the rubbish-pits of summer where raspberries and strawberries burgeon amid the dry brushwood, and wet adders slither beneath the rocks. The air felt oppressive beneath the blanket of grey cloud, but now the wind shifted direction, following the sun, and tumbled the blanket over the horizon; off to the east, bright blue lances were already piercing the cloud cover and the air was shot through with golden glints as if a thousand flashing swords were in motion.

Freed from the darkness and freed from my terror, I could now calmly weigh up the events of the night. I was filled with self-loathing for my lack of courage and composure. The entire thing had been a hallucination, a vision spawned by my agitated senses. And, after all, whose nerves could remain unaffected in times like these? I felt as if I had been wading around in blood.

There was no question of sleep now; I wanted to go down to the sea to hear the noise of the boats casting off and being rowed out to the fishing grounds. I no longer liked the total silence.

The door was not locked. Thank heavens, I thought, that I did not know this last night: it would have been a fresh source of terror.

I walked around the house and over to the window. With my gaze, I measured the distance from the earth to the window frame and quickly concluded that if a man of middling height stood beneath the window, he would reach precisely to the height of the face I had seen against the panes the night before. It was a strange business. Below the window was a little patch of earth, where two wretched apple trees protruded from the black soil, and along the wall ran a flower bed, its flowers sparse and stunted because they always lay in the shade.

I looked at this flowerbed and at once a little waft of the previous night's fear seemed to course through me. In the middle of the flowerbed, clearly impressed upon the black soil, were two footprints. I shoved aside the branches of the trees to take a closer look. Yes, quite so; a person had recently stood on this spot. I placed my left foot beside the prints and when I moved aside, I saw that my foot was just a touch longer than the two footprints, perhaps a half-inch or so. Other than that, there was no difference between the three footprints: they were all

114

equally clear in the soil. And this was precisely what convinced me that a person must have stood here looking through the window very recently, not so many hours before…the previous night? I knelt down and examined the terrain more closely. I found several tracks… I could see where he'd come in, from the road that ran over the flagstone; he'd walked here…and here. Then he'd come into the little patch of garden, bent the branches aside and taken up his station in the middle of the flowerbed. He'd stood here for a long time, several minutes or perhaps half an hour. I could see it from these two footprints, which were deeper than the third. He'd stood there stock-still, looking into my room.

Without knowing quite why, I trampled over the footprints and went on a rampage in the flowerbed with my feet, churning up the earth and snapping the flower stems. When I was finished, I laughed at my own agitation and then I stationed myself close to the wall and looked in through the window.

A tremor ran through me. I was expecting to see something in my room. I imagined that it must look quite different in there now than when I'd left it. I had a presentiment of the same terror that must seize a man when he goes over to a mirror and sees another man's face in its green depths.

But the room was not in the slightest bit different. There stood the table, there the chair, over there the bed; and on the walls hung the same pictures: the oil prints and Norway's Founding Fathers of 1905.

Now I stood and looked through the lowermost pane of the window. I remembered that it was in just this pane I had seen the dead man's face against the ebony-black darkness. And the murdered forestry inspector, Blinde, was exactly the same height as me. It fitted. The dead man had stood outside my window last night.

I hurried away from the house.

The footprints, with their indisputable reality, confused me and turned all my deductions on their head. It had not been a hallucination after all, then. But the forestry inspector was dead, wasn't he? The murdered man was dead and buried, so how could he stand outside my window at night and look in at me?

I set off down the road along the shore, walking with some effort, for although the sun had not yet broken through, the heat lay pressing upon the earth and I knew it would be a crushingly hot day.

There was still not a soul to be seen, but from down on the shore I could hear various noises – bottom boards being put in place, boats being bailed out. The red boathouses seemed redder than usual because the damp sea air of the previous night had heightened their colour. The sea lay absolutely still, stuck fast to the rock face and the skerries. But now a rowing boat glided out of the shadows close to the shore, an old man at the oars, and sliced slowly onwards with groaning oarlocks, sending a fan of ripples out across the whole bay.

As I walked I guessed what time it might be. Four, five? Because these were the signs of life one would hear at that time. Several more boats rowed by. Now I heard voices too, muffled talk somewhere in the vicinity of the jetty.

And as I stood here by the sea, impressions of the day's dawning life flowing towards me; as my thoughts constantly, half-unthinkingly rambled around the eerie events of the night, a sure suspicion began to grow within me. I knew that this suspicion had flickered through my thoughts now and then before, but it had never found a firm foothold until this precise moment. And now it was suddenly there, clear and distinct and unassailable. I could not rid myself of it. I walked back and forth

116

on the jetty, quivering with tension: this was how it must be; this was how it all fitted together. And this was how it could all be explained. It was as if the veil had suddenly been drawn aside from all the mysteries. But at the same time, a hollow feeling of terror came upon me again, a sense that some great danger was close at hand.

I walked up to the hotel. I did not expect to meet any guests but thought I could probably find myself a glass of beer or a cup of broth. After my fainting fit I felt as weak as if I had been on a long fast.

When I reached the lawn that separated the hotel from the road, I saw that the red-striped awning on the veranda had not been rolled up for the night. I went up the steps, walked on to the veranda and peered through the glass door that led into the dining room.

Naturally enough, not a soul was to be seen in the big room. The door was not locked, so I walked in. There was a cloth on the table, with the remains of the evening meal, a scattering of breadcrumbs and half-empty milk glasses beside the place settings; they did not expect guests so early in the morning. In a corner behind some artificial palm trees stood a black piano, grinning with its snow-white keys; I knew that it was there and let my eyes slide over towards it. Above the panelling, a ridiculous array of glasses and cups lined all the walls. By the door out to the kitchen was a counter, and on top of it stood a phonograph and a yellow contraption for uncorking bottles. As soon as I saw this machine, I seemed in my nervous agitation to hear it humming. I was very tired and slid down into a chair beside the window.

Then I heard a creaking over by the piano and my gaze flitted quickly back there again. A terrible shudder ran through me... Good God! There was a man sitting on the piano stool –

how dull I had been, not to notice this person even though I'd actually looked over at the piano.

When I saw who the man was, I felt uneasy despite myself. It was Asbjørn Krag, the detective. He walked over to me, nodding his shining bald head and smiling. All at once, I felt oddly afraid of him and did not want him to come any closer; his face was bony and bloodless, and his smile, which was intended to be amiable and friendly, turned ugly. He walked straight up to me.

'Did you sleep well?' he asked.

And now, as I looked him in the eyes and sensed his gaze upon me, I had a heavy, overwhelming feeling that my suspicions had become reality; they were no longer suspicions: I knew, with a terrible clarity and irrefutable certainty.

As calmly as I was able, I replied, 'Yes, thank you. I slept well.'

Then he reached into his pocket for his watch, and drew it out slowly. It was a golden double hunter. Click, it went, as the case sprang open.

'It is five in the morning.'

'Ah. Yes, I thought as much.'

'It is five in the morning,' repeated the detective. 'And although you may have slept well, you have not slept long, at any rate. Moreover, I can see from your eyes that you have had bad dreams.'

'I had one bad dream,' I replied. 'And it woke me. But why should it surprise you that I am nervous and exhausted, when every day there is some new shock to be endured.'

The detective stood looking at me for a while; a scrutinising, interested look.

'I think you should move back to the hotel,' he said then.

'Why?'

'There are plenty of people here. You have friends and acquaintances here. There really is no need whatsoever for you to live in such isolation.'

'Do you really think I am afraid?'

'I assume that such great isolation must have a depressive effect on you.'

'Not in the least. I like being alone. And I can assure you that I have been disturbed by neither living souls nor phantoms during the time I have lived out there on the headland.'

'Well, well. Really not?'

I could no longer bear the detective's horribly scrutinising gaze. I went out onto the veranda. Shortly afterwards, he was standing by my side.

But now he spoke in a quite different manner, amicable and ingratiating. He could well understand I might wish to get up early to enjoy this splendid day from the very beginning.

'Today, it will be warm throughout the district,' he said, pointing out across the wheat fields. The yellow surface, which rippled gently in the morning sun, spilt over into the forest where the trees stood, trunks deep in wheat.

Asbjørn Krag looked at his watch again.

'What are you waiting for?' I asked.

'For the workers who will drag the iron chariot out of the sea,' he said. 'Have you really forgotten about it already?'

'No. I'm glad the mystery of the iron chariot will be solved at last.'

Shortly afterwards, we heard footsteps inside the hotel. Doors were opened and closed. Declaring that he had an enormous morning appetite, Asbjørn Krag went to track down the landlady and steaming coffee was brought in to us. I tried to eat but it was almost impossible. All the while, I felt Asbjørn Krag's scrutinising gaze upon me.

'You are probably not used to being up so early,' remarked the detective. 'You have no appetite whatsoever.'

'You are right. And now I feel as if I may have slept too little after all. My eyelids are warm and heavy.'

'But you mustn't on any account go to bed,' Krag said eagerly. 'You must come down to the sea with me – the iron chariot will be dragged up. I can promise you an interesting experience. And this time without any blood,' he added in a low voice. 'We have had enough blood, have we not?'

I did not reply.

Asbjørn Krag laughed, a dry crackle of laughter.

'What are you laughing about?'

'I do beg your pardon,' he said. 'Perhaps it's a little heartless of me, but that's just my nature and cannot be helped. I see your fingers shaking, your fork clattering against the plate. I saw your face twitch when I mentioned blood. I find it interesting to observe how the sinister can get a grip on certain people and break them down altogether, little by little.'

'I am not broken down.'

'I did not say that you were, but you are terribly affected by it, that much I can tell.'

'Does that surprise you?'

'On the contrary, my dear fellow; I would have found it much more peculiar if you had gone through all these events without being affected. But I can hear the workers now.'

A carriage came clattering along the road. Asbjørn Krag folded his napkin, placed it calmly beside his plate and went over to the window.

When he got there, he murmured, 'Ah, yes. There they are.'

I went over to the window too.

Down on the road stood a four-wheeler. One man had just jumped out of the carriage, while another held the reins. These two could not be locals for I had never seen them before.

I was standing directly behind Asbjørn Krag and as I was

slightly taller than him, I could see his bald, shining pate. The skin over the crown of his head was white and fine as a new-born babe's and I could see the veins, bluish-green and throbbing to the beat of his pulse. Right there, at the hairline, I thought. That was where the forestry inspector was dealt the mortal blow that smashed the casing of his brain like china. A strange tremor coursed through me and I could not take my eyes off that shining crown and the bluish-green veins. All at once the detective turned around quickly and looked at me.

'My goodness, your eyes!' he said.

I stared straight past him out towards the road. I observed with interest how the horse tried in vain to reach the grass at the edge of the ditch with its muzzle. I stood stock-still; I dared not move and an inexplicable fear sank down in me. But what had I to be afraid of? A thought I had not thought.

It felt like a release to hear Asbjørn Krag's calm, everyday voice again.

'Shall we go then?' he said. 'The workers are waiting.'

I followed him silently out to the carriage and took my place beside him in the back seat. Then we drove through the forest, across the plain and over the rugged slope that ran from the plain down to the sea.

Down there, where the iron chariot had drowned, as Asbjørn Krag put it, there was now a steamship and several smaller boats. People were out in the boats with plumb lines and poles. A winch was at work, I could hear its clatter. The sea lay still and heavy as lead. I could not see the outermost skerries because the morning mist was wafting out towards open sea, concealing them beneath it; the scene was as grey and colourless as a pale charcoal sketch. We walked down to the shore, wading through sand and over tufts of grass. The sand was crusted and damp with dew. The stones were also damp and the vessels out on the water looked sodden. Such is the intensity of the moisture the sea casts up at night.

But the noise carried on the raw morning air as if through a telephone wire. Asbjørn Krag stood on the shore and called out to the people on board the steamer, and even though it lay quite some distance offshore, we heard their replies, clear and ringing.

'Have you found anything?' asked the detective.

'The diver has been down twice,' came the reply from the steamer. 'He's seen a peculiar contraption down on the ocean floor, but it's going to be difficult to haul it up.'

'Is it a carriage?' asked Krag.

'It certainly doesn't look like a carriage,' replied the man on board. 'But it does have wheels, and it's made entirely of iron or steel. The diver has never seen anything like it before.'

'How soon can you haul it out of the sea?'

'Ah, that will take a few hours. It's very heavy.'

The people in the small boats had stood listening to the conversation. Another voice interjected, 'It's lying twenty fathoms deep; we haven't the faintest idea how it got so far out.'

Asbjørn Krag waved and replied: 'It rolled along on the seabed of course. Have you found any passengers?'

After a remarkably long silence, the wondering reply came back: 'No. Was there a passenger on board?'

'Who knows?' Krag answered. 'Search carefully.'

Asbjørn Krag walked a few paces along the water's edge as the work continued in the boats and the winch rattled once more.

I was greatly astonished by the vast machinery that had been set in motion – there must have been twenty to twenty-five men at work.

'Where did all these people come from?' I asked Krag. 'And this boat, how did you get hold of it?'

'It is a diving boat,' answered the detective, 'as you can certainly see. I wired for it yesterday evening. The workers come with the boat.'

He looked across the sea and murmured, half to himself, 'There is no point waiting. They won't be finished for several hours. I'll go back to the hotel for the time being.'

I stood for a while looking out across the sea. The boats lay scattered. If they have found the place where the chariot lies, I thought, why don't they gather all the boats in that spot? Surely that would make it a simple matter to roll the chariot ashore, at least.

I pointed this out to Asbjørn Krag, but he replied, 'Ah, it is a difficult business. The chariot is heavy and large as well.'

Suddenly I remembered what he had said about the passenger.

'Surely you do not think,' I asked, appalled, 'that we shall find yet another dead man?'

'One must always allow for the very worst,' answered Asbjørn Krag. 'Come, let us go. We shall know the truth soon enough.'

The carriage was waiting at the top of the hill and I thought we would drive back to the hotel. But Asbjørn Krag suggested a stroll, to which I had no objection. I was eager to liven myself up with a brisk walk. I could feel the weariness in every limb, but I was too nervous to sleep, that much I knew. My pulse raced in my veins with rapid beats, and awful, silent explosions flared up in my nerves.

Krag was still walking south along the seashore and I followed him. Surely he did not intend to go this way? I said nothing. Some time later, I realised there was a purpose to this stroll that fitted in with the detective's plans. Apparently nothing at all that he did was without some underlying intention. And yet his manner was so normal and everyday that it attracted no attention and he never seemed to be doing anything unusual.

123

'Where are you taking me?' I asked presently.

'Back to the hotel,' he said. 'I will show you a route that you may not have taken before – the road over the hilltop.'

'I didn't even know there was such a road.'

'Ah yes, a fairly broad path that's a pleasure to walk along. It's the perfect road for us on such a delightful, fresh morning.'

He had no eye for nature; he had said the morning was delightful and fresh when it was in fact quiet; quiet and dull, with a low sky and a hazy horizon. The sea was the colour of dynamite and so still that the underwater skerries ventured above the surface. On mornings such as this, fish hurl themselves upon the hook in rage and when you reel them in, their eyes foam with blood; for men, it is suicide weather. I stood on the hilltop and yearned for a fresh wind, a swift breeze to chill my breast. I wet my finger to see which way the wind was blowing. But there was no discernible coolness; the day would be hot and unbearable – I could already feel the heat in my eyes.

The detective stopped in his tracks.

'Now we have reached the top,' he said, pointing over a steep cliff that plunged straight down to the sea.

I walked over to the edge…but rapidly drew back again.

'Does it make you dizzy?'

'Perhaps. At any rate, I don't like looking down into abysses.'

Asbjørn Krag was silent for a while. Now something's coming, I thought, and waited tensely to hear what he would say.

'I have often marvelled,' the detective began, 'at how stupidly murderers tend to behave.'

'Murderers?'

'Yes, and the very worst murderers are the ones who act instinctively, without premeditation. But even the ones who act upon a plan that they have laid out are often infuriatingly clumsy. Take the man who killed the forestry inspector, for

124

example...'

'Are you convinced, then, that he was murdered?'

'Absolutely.'

'I do not understand how you can be so sure of it. Old Gjærnæs and Blinde were found dead on the same spot. Both had a wound to the back of their heads. You said yourself that old Gjærnæs's death was an accident and that the mysterious iron chariot was responsible for his death. Couldn't the same thing be true of the forestry inspector?'

'No. Because I know that he was killed.'

'It will be difficult to prove, at any rate.'

'Very difficult,' replied Asbjørn Krag thoughtfully. 'And that is why I am adopting a most unusual approach to this case. Still, you must at least concede that the murderer behaved very foolishly.'

'I don't know if fool is the correct term for a man who goes about killing other people.'

'Of course not. I meant only to refer to the way the crime was committed. How much easier it would have been to murder him on this spot.'

'Here?'

'Yes, indeed. Imagine if the murderer had possessed enough self-control to be able to walk along this road, calmly chatting with his victim, just as we are chatting now. Then he could simply have given him a shove, a light tap on the shoulder, and he would have tumbled off and been killed. And who do you suppose would have thought of murder in that case? An accident, people would have said, a tragic accident. Or perhaps suicide.'

'But what about the man who was walking with him?' I whispered.

'He was walking alone. Nobody need know that the murderer

125

went walking with his victim. Few people stroll along this road. It is possible to make one's way onto it from the boathouses without anybody noticing.'

The detective laughed out loud.

'So now you have heard how easy it is to be a murderer if one is familiar with the terrain. But my dear fellow,' he continued, clapping me on the shoulder, 'I have come back around to the same sinister subject as ever. Still, that is my task after all – it is part of my life's work to be constantly thinking about these matters. But I shall try to avoid talking about it when I am in your company. I can see that you find it thoroughly disagreeable.'

In a voice that seemed to come from some place oddly deep down in my throat, I replied, 'You may talk to me about whatever you want. So you think that the murderer could have committed his crime in absolute safety if he had done it that way?'

'Ah no, my dear fellow,' interrupted Krag, in a most amiable voice. 'You simply must not encourage me to talk about this matter again. It is far too polite of you: I know you do not like it.'

With that, he walked onwards, several paces ahead of me. He dipped his head a little and the collar of his jacket curled up towards his neck. It seemed to me that he was chuckling.

When we arrived back at the hotel, Asbjørn Krag went straight into his room to work. I wandered around for a while, talking to the other guests. All of them were planning to go and watch the iron chariot being dragged up. Reports of the diving company's arrival had circulated and it was said that the diver had already been down several times to look at the chariot, but that he was not yet entirely certain what it actually was. They wished me to join them, but I did not want to. I thought about the passenger, the dead passenger. And I pictured him to myself, lying down there in the green water. Perhaps at this very moment he was being drawn slowly through the ocean – ah, how clearly I could see his face in the sea. As if it were gliding up towards a green windowpane. A desperate thought struck me… Asbjørn Krag's room was on the ground floor of the hotel, and his window looked out over a little patch of garden, just as mine did. I knew he was sitting in there working at his desk, face turned towards the windowpane.

I crept in beneath the branches as quietly as I was able, then suddenly stood upright, outside his window. At once, I saw his white pate against the dark backdrop of the room. He was not writing, but working on something that lay before him on the table. He had not heard me. I walked closer, slowly and carefully. This, I thought, is just how the dead man's face glided towards my window last night. When I was an arm's length or so from the window, he heard the sound of twigs snapping beneath my feet. He raised his head abruptly and I saw his sudden astonishment. I said nothing, but brought my face ever closer to the windowpane. He quickly seized a newspaper and spread it out across the desk. It struck me at once that he was hiding something from me; there was something I must not on any account see – that much I understood from his quick, nervous movements. And I had not expected that. All at once, the absurdity of my behaviour became clear to me. What did I want with him?

He opened the window.

'Can I help you with anything?' he asked.

I said the first thing that came into my head. 'Won't you be going to look for the iron chariot soon?'

'Not yet. But if you have some special interest in going there, I will gladly accompany you.'

'No, thank you,' I said. 'No special interest.'

I wanted to withdraw. I felt humiliated and ridiculed, and

became even angrier with myself when he said: 'Poor man. You are quite pale. Haven't you slept yet?'

'I do not generally sleep in the middle of the morning,' I replied.

The detective closed his window, but did not remove the concealing newspaper from the table as long as I was able to see into the room.

I drifted away from the hotel and walked quickly but aimlessly along the road. Now the sun had rolled up into the sky. My footsteps stirred up dust that rose into the air like loose flour.

At the dinner table, there was much eager chatter about the iron chariot. The diving boat had not yet managed to haul it up and people thought that it would take the whole day.

One of the ladies, who knew the family of the murdered forestry inspector, offered some information that affected me greatly.

She had received a letter from the dead man's sister. The forestry inspector had a dog called Lord. Since the funeral, Lord had been lying on his dead master's grave, howling and barking as if to summon him back to life. In the end, the dog had to be shot.

After dinner, I tried to sleep out on the grass, but the terrible light streaming down from the sky disturbed me. When I shut my eyes, their lids glowed red. I looked up at the sky; the air was a sea of diamonds. I went home to my cabin.

But here a fresh surprise awaited me. I could not help looking at the spot beneath the window. Driven by nervous curiosity, I was forced to go there. Before I had left the place that morning, I had churned up the earth and erased the two footprints. But now the prints were back again: two distinct footprints in the loose soil. I examined them carefully. They were exactly like the earlier ones; they were the dead man's footprints. He had been here and looked in through my window in my absence.

I hurried into my room. I did not want to think about this any longer, I was afraid I was going mad. Was the murdered man not dead, then? But I had seen his body in the sand-digger's hut after all. He had been buried and his dog shot... And now, too, I seemed to hear a dog baying, somewhere far off in the distance – a peculiar, mournful baying. I shut the window and rolled down the blind so that the room was in semi-darkness. I wanted to sleep, regardless.

I slept for a fairly long time, but was woken by a sinister dream. I thought I was standing before a mirror examining my own face, which was pale and sickly. As my eyes fell upon my tie, it seemed to change colour. Originally blue, it suddenly became green, the same colour as the dead man's tie. I noted this with astonishment and interest, although without actually becoming afraid. But then suddenly the tie moved: the knot loosened and slid to one side, until in the end it was pushed up towards my right ear, exactly as it had been on the dead man. My eyes – this is how I dreamt it – were still fixed only on the tie. I could not see anything else. And now the terror suddenly came washing over me: if I shifted my gaze, I would see the face, but would it still be my pale, sickly face in the mirror or that of another man? All at once, the whole figure in the mirror slid slowly downwards and now I saw a reddish-brown beard, now I saw a pink mouth. And there was the face: the dead man with the high forehead, chalk-white against an ebony background. As I woke, I heard a scream – my own.

By now it was nine o'clock in the evening. It was suppertime, but I hadn't the faintest desire for food and did not want to leave the cabin. Since I did not want to roll up the blind either, I had to light the lamp. I read several pages of a book absent-mindedly, with no awareness of what I was actually reading.

The words passed before my consciousness like torrential rain before a window. A couple of hours passed in this way and then, all at once, I heard steps in the sand outside the walls of the house. The steps were not heading towards the door, but the window.

I got up quickly and reached for my revolver. The steps stopped. But then I heard one footstep and then another, closer. It was a terrible feeling, to stand in the cabin and not know who was walking around outside. But still, it was quite usual to hear footsteps outside the cabin; I was in a densely populated bathing resort after all. I remember that I thought about this and despised myself for my fear, but I was so agitated and nervous by now that the slightest unexpected noise was all it took to utterly disconcert me.

After this, I did not hear anything for some time, but then I noticed somebody fumbling at the outer wall of the cabin. There was something odd about this fumbling, as if some furry creature were rubbing its carcass against the wall. Then everything went quiet again for a few seconds, and after that I heard hard, bony knuckles knocking at the door.

The door was not locked.

'Come in,' I cried, in a voice quite unrecognisable to me.

The door opened and Asbjørn Krag came quickly into the room.

When he caught sight of me with the revolver in my hand, he stopped dead.

'Oh, you've really gone too far this time!' he said. 'You are far too nervous now. Do you really think somebody wants to see you dead?'

I threw the revolver onto the table.

'You have a peculiar way of arriving,' I said. 'Why did you go past the window?'

'I couldn't remember where the door was.'

It seemed to me that he was smiling. In any event, I could see the white teeth which made that angular face of his so sinister.

'So was that you fumbling along the side of the house?'

'Yes. I was trying to find the door.'

Krag sat down at the table and picked up my revolver. He weighed it appraisingly in his hand and checked the magazine.

'I see all the chambers are loaded,' he said. 'It's a splendid weapon. Are you a good shot?'

'Yes, very good.'

Presently, he put the weapon down.

'Is there something on your mind, Mr Krag?'

'Yes,' the detective replied. 'I just wanted to ask you whether you would like to see the iron chariot.'

'Have they dragged it out of the water now?'

'Yes.'

'And the passenger?' I asked, in a whisper.

'We have also found the passenger. He is dead.'

'I had actually been thinking about going to sleep just now,' I replied.

'Now you are afraid.'

'Not in the least.'

The detective narrowed his eyes at me. His gaze, with its blend of malice and *schadenfreude*, enraged me and I said, 'In any event you are doing your utmost to frighten me. It must be irritating for you to see your efforts fail like this, time after time.'

'Now I cannot make head or tail of what you are saying,' answered Asbjørn Krag.

'Of course you went past my window intentionally. And I am certain there was some purpose to it when you scraped against the wall like some kind of animal.'

'But I have explained the reason for these phenomena. You

are far too nervous, my dear fellow – you see and hear ghosts everywhere. Isn't it only too natural for a person to fumble around a little in the dark before finding the doorknob?'

'It isn't even especially dark tonight.'

'Ah yes it is. The sky is overcast and lies low upon the earth.'

But I was determined to show the detective my disapproval.

'You did it on purpose,' I said. 'You were padding around out there like an animal, like a wolf.'

Asbjørn Krag did not answer straight away. He sat down at the table, picked up my revolver and let the beautiful weapon slip playfully through his fingers.

Presently he murmured thoughtfully: 'Aha, so that's what it sounded like...like an animal, as if a wolf were walking back and forth outside, padding around.'

'Yes, or a dog.'

'Did you hear the dog this evening?'

The detective looked at the window, where the blind was gently stirring in the draught from the cracks in the window frame.

'Did you hear the dog?' he repeated.

'Which dog?'

'The dog.'

He spoke quite calmly, but still there was a slight ring of impatience in his voice, as if to say: My dear fellow, there can be no dog other than the one I am referring to. And you know quite well which dog it is.

I sat, rocking slowly in the rocking chair. I lowered my head so that the detective could not see my face.

I thought about the dead man's dog. The distant barking still echoed in my ears; there was something peculiar and menacing in the dog's mournful howling.

After a silence that lasted several minutes, I said, 'I heard a dog barking a while ago. Is that the one you mean?'

'Yes,' answered the detective.

After that, he simply sat and listened. The beam of the lamp fell directly upon his face, making it white and translucent. I stopped the rocking chair and looked at him. I was profoundly contented with the thought that I myself was sitting in the shadow, while his face was sharply illuminated. The detective was leaning his right elbow on the table. I observed his hand closely: it was thin and very hairy at the wrist; the fingers were long and bony, with bluish skin… But why did he sit this way, listening? Now I felt myself grow nervous again. It was as if this intent listening of his warned me that a third person was present in the room, an unknown, unseen being. And then the silence… Again there was this silence that I had been so intensely aware of that morning out on the plain. The silence that you should not listen out for, because then all you will hear is a tumult of strange noises, myriad shrieks and, in the end, a distant, heavy rumbling that is not of this world… I needed to hear voices; I wanted to hear my own voice.

'What are you listening out for?' I asked.

He held up his hand in warning.

'Hush, I think I hear…'

'What do you hear?'

He didn't answer. He was still listening.

And now it came at last. A sad and plaintive sound. It was the dog.

I rose so quickly from the rocking chair that the decrepit old thing creaked.

'I cannot bear to hear that dog barking… Ah, that terrible howling. Do you hear it, Krag? The dog cannot be far away.'

Now Asbjørn Krag got up too. He brought his face close to mine. I felt as if I had fallen right into his eyes.

'Do you know the dog?' he asked.

'No. But there are a great many dog-owners living here, after all.'

'I have never heard a dog howling like that down here before,' said Asbjørn Krag. 'I heard the dog when I was on my way here, too. And it stopped me in my tracks. I tried to find out where the sound was coming from, but I could not; it constantly shifted position.'

'That's the way…' I whispered. 'That's the way dogs howl when somebody is about to die.'

Asbjørn Krag was still listening.

Now the sad, plaintive howl became a menacing baying.

Asbjørn Krag seized me by the arm.

'It is a hunting dog,' he said.

'Can you tell that from the sound?'

'Yes, from its bark. And there aren't any hunting dogs for dozens of miles around here as far as I know.'

I did not notice how absurd his words were, for I was in thrall to a peculiar, eerie atmosphere. And he made me shiver when he said, 'The murdered man's dog was also a hunting dog.'

'Yes, but it has been shot,' I said.

'Indeed, because they could not keep it away from its master's grave. It lay howling on the tomb to summon him back to life again. And I imagine that it must have howled and wailed just like the dog we can hear now.'

I did not answer. Presently, the detective said: 'Imagine, my dear fellow, just imagine if we are the only two who can hear it. Imagine if no other living soul can hear it.'

I was perturbed, but struggled to control my agitation and said, 'It seems to me that you are the one who is conjuring up ghosts now.'

Asbjørn Krag buttoned up his jacket.

'Think over what I have said.'

Oddly enough, the dog stopped barking at that very moment.

'Are you leaving?'

'Yes. I shall go down to look at the iron chariot and its dead passenger.'

Both the iron chariot and the dead passenger had slipped my mind entirely, so absorbed had I been by the dog. But now this new reality suddenly sank in: the iron chariot had been found and the passenger was dead.

'Was he killed too?' I asked.

'No.'

'So was his death an accident?'

'Yes. Just like old Gjærnæs. There is only one person who has been murdered here: the forestry inspector.'

'Are you still certain of that?'

'Yes. He was killed on a night just like this, when grey clouds flit beneath the heavens.'

'You are tragic this evening, Asbjørn Krag.'

The detective smiled.

'I am, in fact, something of a poet,' he said. 'A poet of fear. Will you come with me?'

I gave it some thought.

Should I go with him or stay behind? It was vital not to give the detective the impression that I was afraid.

'I think there is little point,' I said, 'in my seeing yet another body. But I shall gladly accompany you because I'm interested in the iron chariot. Have you seen it?'

'Yes.'

'Were you surprised?'

'No. It was just as I had imagined it over the past few days.'

'Do you think I shall be surprised?'

'Yes. Are you coming?'

135

'I'm coming.'

The detective went over to the table and picked up my revolver.

'You will bring this little item with you, of course,' he said.

'Why?'

'For safety's sake. I think you are a little scared. You might, for example, meet a dog along the way.'

A derisive smile lit up his face again. The detective bared his teeth.

'I am not afraid,' I said. 'Leave the revolver here.'

He looked at the revolver more closely.

It really is a beautiful weapon,' he murmured. He opened the magazine.

'All the chambers are loaded, I see.'

'Of course it's loaded. What point would there be in having the weapon otherwise?'

'You could frighten people with it,' answered the detective. 'You have no idea how far you can get by frightening people.'

I opened the door.

'Shall we go, then?' I said.

The detective put the gun down on the table and followed me.

When we were a few paces away from the cabin, I heard the detective laugh – a dry, unpleasant laugh.

'What are you laughing at?'

'The lamp,' he said. 'The lamp in your cabin is lit again.'

'Yes, it was sheer forgetfulness on my part.'

'For the second time. Ah well, you may just as well leave it lit. That way, you'll be spared the trouble of lighting it when you get home.'

I wanted to take the road that passed by the hotel, but Asbjørn Krag stopped me.

'Not that road,' he said. 'It's quicker to walk over the hilltop.'

He wanted to walk the same route we had taken that morning. I remembered his sinister chatter during that walk and shuddered.

By now it was quite dark and not a soul was in sight. We walked quickly past the small, dead houses and onto the hilltop road.

'There, you can see it for yourself,' said Asbjørn Krag. 'Nobody has seen us together. Now if one of us were to vanish...'

I must have made an involuntary movement, for the detective broke off.

'Don't you like this?'

'No, I see no point in that kind of talk.'

The detective took me by the arm. He said, in an almost comradely ingratiating tone, 'But my dear fellow, it is so long since we have talked of such matters that you must allow me to be a little tactless now. I have a personal interest in convincing you. Before long now we shall reach the place where a murder like that could be committed. One would need only give one's companion a nudge – and down he would tumble into the abyss. It is very simple, is it not? And nobody would ever find out about it either. And if the body were found, there would not even be any talk of murder because it would be clear as day that it could only have been an accident.'

I tried again to interrupt him, but without success.

He continued unmoved.

'Ha ha! Yes, now you will laugh of course, but I believe the comparison is far too good to waste. Imagine that I hated you for some reason or another. Is that impossible to contemplate?'

'I can hardly believe that,' I muttered. My thoughts were a long way off. I was yearning for my peaceful cabin. I felt that our adventure was already taking a quite sinister turn.

'But of course such a thing is thinkable,' continued Asbjørn Krag. 'You can draw on examples from all conceivable relationships. It is quite possible to imagine I might hate you for some reason or another. Let us suppose that you knew something about me that could cause me terrible harm if you were to tell anybody else about it. Don't you think I might hate you then? I would almost certainly hate you so much that I would wish you dead. And you must admit, then, that it might very easily occur to me to push you into the abyss on just such a walk as this.'

'What strange things you say,' I said. 'Once again, I simply cannot understand you.'

'I believe I have presented the matter quite clearly.'

'Or too clearly,' I replied. 'My dear Asbjørn Krag, there is no use denying it. I'm convinced now that there is some particular purpose to your behaviour.'

Now he laughed again, that same dry, unpleasant laugh.

'What might my purpose be, then?' he asked.

'That I really do not know.'

But I did know. I knew it all too well. I suspected the whole truth.

We were approaching the abyss – the place where one need only give a little nudge to the person one wished to be rid of. The abyss lay to the left of the road and all this time I had been walking to the right of Asbjørn Krag.

'Here it is,' he said, and stopped.

We were buffeted by a cold gust from the abyss and the sea.

'Aren't we going to carry on?' I asked.

Instead of answering, Asbjørn Krag pointed down at the sea, where a couple of green lanterns shone in the darkness like cats' eyes.

'Down there lies the iron chariot, which has been dragged

up onto the shore. And on the deck of the rescue ship, wrapped in sailcloth, lies the dead passenger. Doesn't it look eerie, with those green lanterns? And yet up here it is quite still, not a sound reaches us up here from down below... But yes...down there he lies, the dead man.'

'Do you know him?' I asked in a whisper.

'No, and nor do you. He is a blank stranger.'

'That is most peculiar.'

'When you see the chariot, you will find it all makes perfect sense.'

'And it is him, this stranger, who has been driving around in the iron chariot at night?'

'Yes, but only for the past few days. He has scarcely driven over the plain more than four or five times.'

'This is a mystery. But did he drive over the plain the night when...when the forestry inspector died?'

'Yes, he did. When the forestry inspector was killed, he was not far away. But you will understand all of this when you see the iron chariot.'

A little later I asked, 'Were you there when they found the passenger?'

'Yes, I saw him being pulled up out of the water. It was not a pleasant sight. His face was so oddly pale down there in the water. He looked... Well now, what did he actually look like?... Have you ever seen a corpse through a green glass windowpane?'

At the detective's last words I gave a violent start.

All at once it was as if I could see the dead man's face again, behind my windowpane...the white forehead...the pink lips... A great shudder of fear ran through me and for a tenth of a second I relived the previous night's terror. And, as if from afar, I heard Asbjørn Krag's voice say, 'Shall we go on? That way you shall see him for yourself in a moment.'

But now I did not want to go down there, not for all the world. The green lanterns reminded me of the phosphorus glint in the eye-sockets of a skull.

I turned back.

'I'm not going down there,' I said. 'I want to go back home to my cabin.'

I walked a few paces then stopped all at once.

Far off in the darkness, I heard the dog again. A high, shrill baying, then a long howl and then long, menacing barks.

'The hunting dog,' said Asbjørn Krag's voice. 'Do you hear the hunting dog?'

The barking continued.

It sounded so infinitely distant; it came from the very darkness beyond the horizon. I listened out for it; it grew louder, then became muffled and feeble, but steadily more menacing. In the end, it was as if the barking filled the whole of the eastern sky. I felt as if terror itself were breathing out of the darkness. But still there was something in this dark baying that called to me, commanding. I walked onwards.

But then I heard Asbjørn Krag's voice right beside me.

'Do not follow the sound!' he cried.

The muffled barking settled around me like a woollen mist and quite confused me. I felt that terror lay in the very air, breathing upon me with its warm breath… I walked towards the sound, unaware of what I was doing. As I came down towards the houses, the barking seemed to become more distant again, dipping below the horizon. Shortly afterwards, it stopped completely. I was quite alone now. Asbjørn Krag had left me and walked on down to the iron chariot, down towards the green corpse. I walked more and more quickly in my eagerness to reach my cabin.

When I drew close to the cabin, where the open sea spread

140

out before me, I saw a strange, white light shining on the sea. There was something spectral about this light; it seemed so peculiar, surrounded as it was by stillness and the grey-black darkness. It didn't even occur to me that it was the first white strip of daybreak glittering on the surface of the sea.

The lamp was still burning.

I was terribly agitated by now. My nerves exploded in thousands of small, burning pinpricks around my body.

I was glad that the blind was down. That way the room seemed to be shut off from the world. After rooting about aimlessly in my papers for a while, I sat down in the rocking chair. That calmed me somewhat, because when the rocking chair was empty I felt as if somebody was sitting in it whenever my face was turned away. I wanted to occupy that place.

I sat for a time, rocking and thinking, my eyes fixed all the while upon the revolver that lay on the table, glinting at me. I wondered how many more hours I could live this life before going mad.

Then I heard the tick of the death-watch beetle again.

This time, it did not frighten me, although the sound constantly shifted position and swarmed around me like an irritable insect. It was just as if some invisible person were walking around, a person I could not see, but whose pocket watch I could hear. Now the person was there... Now they walked slowly over to the right... Now they stood still over by the lamp. For a second the sheen of my revolver seemed to dim, as if a shadow was about to seize it. But then the revolver glinted again, steel-cold as before, and then the death-watch beetle seemed to move away. No, this did not frighten me in the least; on the contrary, I felt safer because I knew the reason for this phenomenon.

Why was it so urgent for Asbjørn Krag to show me the iron

chariot and the dead stranger tonight? I recalled his strange conversation along the way, when he'd wanted to intimidate me into listening to his explanations of how a murderer should behave. Time after time now he had wanted to take me to the place where all it would take was a nudge – a quite small, unexpected movement – to send some troublesome fellow mortal tumbling into the hereafter.

And why did he leave me when I turned my face towards the eastern skies and followed the sound?

Followed the sound… Now I remembered the barking again, and shuddered tremulously as my senses resounded to the echo of that muffled, terrible animal cry. Of course it had been the dog on one of the farms – yes, I was sure of it; but even so, I couldn't help thinking of the forestry inspector's dead hunting dog. I saw it in my mind's eye, with its long, silken-soft coat and great, wondering eyes. At that moment, I could well understand how I might feel the barking was calling to me, warning me.

Abruptly, I stopped the slow rocking of my chair and sat there, listening with wide-open ears.

I had caught a sound outside my window: a branch snapping, a faint rustling in the undergrowth. It was not the wind. It sounded as if long fingers were slipping through the leaves.

Immediately afterwards, there was a knock on the windowpane – a hard rap. I had heard that sound before. It must be a bird, I thought, that had hurtled towards the light and struck its beak on the windowpane.

But presently I heard again a knocking on the pane; this time, there were two hard raps that made me think of knuckles.

I leapt up and seized the revolver, felt its ice-cold haft in my hand. Now I no longer had any doubt about it: I knew what I would do.

With a rapid movement, I would snap open the blind.

Already, in advance, I had a sense of how things would unfold. As soon as I could see the coal-black windowpane, I would leap backwards. A fleeting image ran nervily through my mind: an animal-tamer in a zoo, opening the cage-door then dashing out of the path of the great, mysterious beast as it starts to run. Now came another knock at the window – this time hard and menacing.

I seized the cord that secured the blind, gave it a quick tug and then released it. The blind shot up with a slap.

I tumbled backwards into the room.

There in the lowermost ebony-black pane was the face again: ghastly and distinct, its pink lips and chalk-white brow shining upon me.

But this time, I did not hide my face. I walked towards my terror, I walked towards the window, possessed by a great and hate-filled will. I saw nothing but this face, felt the revolver in my hand, sensed the wild, embittered rage rising to my head. I wanted to cry out – an oath, a curse – but could not; an indistinct gurgle filled my mouth, as if I were chewing blood.

Then I took aim at the face with my revolver, as close as possible to the windowpane, and fired.

There was a click.

The bright little metallic sound hammered into my brain like a nail.

I fired again.

Again, a click.

And the dreadful face was still there, calm as ever, at the window: it did not move a muscle, its eyelids did not fall but the eyes stared at me, white and dead.

I shot for a third time.

The same click, the same frightful feeling as if a nail were being driven through my nerves.

But now the face became less distinct; the pink turned grey, and little by little, the chalk-white brow was erased. I let the revolver sink. Gradually, the face disappeared, buried by the darkness that closed before it like a thick, black curtain. In the end, I could see nothing but the darkness and the pale reflection in the uppermost panes of that strange, white light from the sea.

I stood there for a long time, staring at the windowpane, bewildered by what I had experienced.

Then I examined the revolver, opened the magazine.

The magazine was empty; all the bullets had been removed.

VII

The Abyss

THE NEXT DAY, I MET ASBJØRN KRAG with a bundle of newspapers under his arm.

He showed me a German paper and said, 'There's something in here about the iron chariot.'

I just nodded.

But then, feeling that my lack of interest was too remarkable, I asked, 'So what does it say about the iron chariot?'

The detective calmly put the newspaper in his pocket.

'Many people around here still have no idea about the secret of the iron chariot. And yet in Berlin one can read about the whole business in the morning paper. Strange, don't you think?'

'Quite unbelievable,' I said. 'How can that be?'

'Why, somebody has wired the Berlin newspapers, naturally.'
'From here?'

'Yes, from here or the nearest telegraph office.'

'Who can it have been?'

'Haven't you guessed yet?' asked Asbjørn Krag, with a laugh.

'No.'

'I was the one who wired, of course,' he said.

'So might I know,' I asked, 'what the secret of this iron chariot actually is?'

'Are you really so terribly interested?'

'Yes.'

'Then why haven't you already driven down there to look at it? The guest house is quite empty – all the other guests have already gone there.'

'I have been writing a couple of important letters,' I began.

'And I dare say you have other matters to think about. More serious matters.'

'Possibly.'

'Would it be indiscreet to ask what they are?'

'First and foremost,' I replied. 'I am thinking of leaving tomorrow.'

A meditative expression crossed the detective's face.

'As soon as tomorrow?' he murmured. 'That may be a little early, but we shall see.'

'What do you mean by that? Are you also thinking of leaving?'

'Possibly, and in that case we can travel together. In all honesty, that would be a pleasure. I do like to have some sensible person to chat to even when I am not working.'

The detective asked me to accompany him to the steamship jetty. The boat was waiting.

I was very surprised by this, because I knew that Asbjørn Krag usually showed no interest in the steamship – unlike the other bathing guests, who looked forward to its arrival tremendously. But now the detective was probably waiting for something; perhaps one of his colleagues was due to arrive.

The white steamer sliced through the water and glided slowly in towards the jetty, which was almost deserted. The shipping agent and his people bustled about, manhandling crates and barrels. A few new summer guests came ashore from the steamboat, mostly women with children and perambulators, as well as some menfolk – a bespectacled gentleman, his skin pale from reading and city dust, and two other young fellows, who looked like sporty types.

I particularly noticed these two. They seemed to be in a hurry, did not greet anybody and had no baggage, although they did have two bicycles with them. They disappeared off along the country road in a cloud of dust.

'Do you know them?' asked Krag.

'Not at all,' I replied. 'Never seen them before.'

'But it seemed to me that you observed the gentlemen with some attention.'

'Quite by chance.'

'Naturally. Well, forgive my curiosity; I do delight in taking note of everything, even the most insignificant things. And just now I saw a little glint in your eyes that led me to suspect that you recognised the gentlemen.'

'But then we would, of course, have greeted one another.'

'Now, now – you know it is quite possible for people to know one another without being on hat-tipping terms.'

'But what about yourself, Krag?' I asked. 'What is your business down here at the jetty?'

'I simply felt like walking down to look at the steamboat,' he said. 'Look, it's casting off again now, so the pleasure is at an end.'

He was lying of course; I realised that at once. Asbjørn Krag always went about hiding his true intentions from me.

Now he wanted me to accompany him to the iron chariot, and I decided to go with him.

'Shall we walk over the hill?' I asked.

'No,' he said. 'We might just as well take the country road. The sun will be baking hot on the hilltop today.'

I could have told him that the sun would be just as hot on the country road, but I let it pass. Of course there was also some purpose to his decision not to take the hilltop path today. I had no desire to ask him about it.

We walked quickly because our trip would need to take less than one and a half hours if we were to be back in time for dinner.

Along the way, he referred to my peculiar behaviour of the previous day.

'I see now how necessary it is,' he said, 'for you to leave this place. I regret having involved you so deeply in this sinister business. And I could tell yesterday that you were genuinely afraid.'

'Of what?'

'Of the man in the iron chariot. You ran away from me, didn't you? Perhaps you wouldn't have been so afraid if you had taken it with you after all.'

'It? What are you talking about?'

'Your revolver, of course.'

I stopped and looked at him. In my heart I had to admire his nerve. He appeared to have forgotten the dog's howls and all the rest of it now. Yet he was the one who had driven me into this sinister state with all his talk about the dead hunting dog. And now he was behaving as if it were nothing at all. His face was just as smooth as ever and his entire manner was obliging, almost beaming with amiability.

'I hope to be able to prove to you,' I said, 'that I will not be afraid at the critical moment.'

'I think you will too; I do not think it is in your nature to be

148

frightened in the least, but all these sinister experiences have left you shaken and uncertain. I do hope you slept well last night.'

'Splendidly.'

We walked along side by side in silence for a while. Then I asked: 'Won't you tell me what it says in the German paper, so that I will at least be slightly prepared.'

'All will become clear to you shortly. I have a weakness for theatricality, I'm fond of little surprises. But this much I have already told you: the iron chariot has nothing whatsoever to do with the murder.'

'The murder of the forestry inspector?'

'Yes. There is no other murder. But through accidental associations other events got entangled in it – first and foremost the iron chariot and then the death of the old man.'

'I dare say you have disentangled all the threads now?'

'Yes. The mystery of old Gjærnæs is already solved. By unlucky chance, he was killed by the iron chariot just as he was fleeing over the plain, with the intention of disappearing again. The same unhappy chance also drove the man in the iron chariot to his death.'

'But what was the man in the iron chariot doing out on the plain that night?'

Asbjørn Krag slapped the bundle of newspapers.

'It is all described here,' he said. 'The man in the iron chariot is the most distinguished of the three dead men. According to the German papers, his death will be a great loss to science. Haven't you read the papers at all lately, my dear fellow?'

'No,' I replied. 'When I'm on holiday, I take no interest in the outside world.'

'Well, I don't know whether the report has reached the Norwegian papers in any case. I took the trouble to send it to the German papers myself. The man in the iron chariot is

German.'

We were now approaching the place where the woods opened out onto the slope that led from the plain down to the sea.

When we eventually got there and looked down, I was amazed at the quantity of people gathered on the shoreline; the ladies' dresses shimmered white and the yellow straw hats glinted. The diving ship still lay out in the bay, but now it had gathered all the small boats to it, like a mother hen gathering her chicks.

The crowd was gazing curiously at an astonishing object that had been pulled up onto the beach. From a distant, it looked like one great snarled mass of iron rods and wheels.

When I came closer, I thought that it must be the wreck of a little steamboat, for I identified two propellers and thought I could see the steamer's shining deck.

I communicated my guess to Asbjørn Krag, but he just laughed and told me to go a little closer. And when I found myself in the midst of the crowd of curious gawpers, I saw at once what it was.

It was neither a steamboat nor an iron chariot.

In fact, there was barely any iron in the wreckage. What I had taken for iron rods proved to be slender rods of nickel and aluminium.

It was a flying machine, a monoplane. What I had assumed to be the steamer's deck were the machine's rigid wings.

Asbjørn Krag seized my arm.

'Do you understand now?' he asked.

'Yes,' I replied. 'Now I understand the whole thing.'

'It was the flying machine we heard that night; it was the flying machine, flying so low that it killed old Gjærnæs. And it was also the flying machine you heard on that sinister night of the murder. Now you understand the buzzing that circled

150

around us, the workings of the machine in the darkness. Now you also understand why it never left any tracks.'

As Asbjørn Krag spoke, all the gawpers gathered in a huddle around him. He did not appear to be in the least bit embarrassed to find himself the object of such general attention. He drew me out of the crowd.

'Let us walk along the beach a little,' he said. 'Then I shall tell you everything.'

The others understood his manoeuvre and did not follow us.

Asbjørn Krag explained, 'It was precisely the accident with old Gjærnæs that brought about the flying machine's destruction. These marvellous, elegant contraptions are not yet so fully developed that they cannot be sent off balance by an unexpected collision of this kind. So that is why the machine spun off down the slope and flew straight into the sea. I imagine that the pilot tried to recover his equilibrium, but failed. So he died at his post, like a captain on his bridge.'

'But I simply don't understand,' I objected, 'why he was carrying out his experiments up here.'

'I shall explain that to you,' answered Krag as he began unfolding some of the foreign newspapers.

'Here is the Evening News for 24th August. A small notice reports the following brief facts: "It is rumoured that renowned German aviator Dr Brahms has made a truly remarkable discovery in the field of aviation technology. The nature of this discovery is as yet unknown, but according to reports from informed sources, the doctor is eagerly engaged in conducting his experiments. However, since aviation secrets have been stolen on several occasions in the past, Dr Brahms has moved his tests to a sparsely populated location and has surrounded his activities in the utmost secrecy. To this end, the parts of his flying machine were transported in large crates marked

'Bechstein grand piano'. According to one rumour, the doctor is making use of the light summer nights in the Nordic region, and conducts his experiments while others are sleeping."

'This was the item that first attracted my attention,' said Asbjørn Krag. 'And now you shall hear what I wired myself.'

Asbjørn Krag read on, as he pulled a German newspaper from the bundle: 'We have received a report from a random correspondent, which will – if there is any truth in it – be a source of grief and regret in wide circles. The report runs thus: "Last night the pilot, Dr Brahms, who has been conducting his test flights in this locality unbeknownst to all, met with an accident. His machine collided with an obstacle and plummeted into the sea after losing control. A diving boat has been summoned to salvage the machine."

'And there you have the entire mystery,' said the detective.

I thought the whole business sounded most peculiar. Had I not seen the smashed-up flying machine for myself, I would scarcely have believed the report.

'When you think it over,' continued Asbjørn Krag, 'you must be amazed at how much simpler everything now becomes. The mysterious iron chariot has vanished. Now you understand how the noise was produced, and you also understand the unhappy accident with old Gjærnæs.'

'And the forestry inspector.'

The detective wrinkled his brow.

'Not at all,' he replied. 'I have already told you that the forestry inspector was killed.'

'It will be difficult for you to prove it after this.'

'Yes, it will be very difficult,' murmured Asbjørn Krag, thoughtfully. 'Nonetheless, I shall manage it in the end.'

'It could take a long time,' I remarked casually.

'For others, perhaps. But not for me.'

'That's an impressive claim, my dear Krag. So how long will it be before you go and point out your man?'

The detective sniffed, nose in the air, as if to draw wisdom from the heavens.

'Within twelve hours,' he said.

'So are you sure that you will get the right man?'

'Absolutely sure.'

'And will you show him to me?'

'Yes,' replied the detective, giving me an odd look, 'if you absolutely insist on seeing him.'

'He isn't dead then?'

'No, he is still alive.'

We walked back the same way we had come. I wanted to press Asbjørn Krag on the matter, to question him about the murderer, but he gave only evasive answers.

I studied his face very closely and it seemed to me that a somewhat tired and tense air had come over him. He had quite certainly grown paler: the skin on his temples and along his hairline was white. He must have been doing some strenuous brainwork lately; perhaps he'd had a lot of sleepless nights.

But how must I look myself? I had not had a sound night's sleep for many days. I could feel the skin around my eyes burning, my lips quivering. My nerves were now entirely worn out. Oh, how I yearned for a long rest. But now, at least, it would soon be over. The boat would leave tomorrow and regardless of whether or not the detective was mistaken, I would leave this terrible place.

As we walked, the detective returned again to the odd circumstance that the whole case had appeared so mysterious at first because three different cases had become entangled with one another.

'If I had not thought to separate out the different events,' he said, 'I dare say I would still be poking about in the darkness.'

This gave me an opportunity to raise the matter of the murder again. 'A long time ago, you told me you could walk over and point out the criminal.' I said. 'Since you were so certain of your case, why didn't you arrest your man long ago?'

'Because I lacked proof. I repeat that I have adopted a quite unusual approach in this case.'

The detective stopped, and looked at me with narrowed eyes.

'I have waited for the fruit to ripen,' he said.

'And is it now ripe?'

'Soon. In a matter of hours. Then it will drop straight into my hands.'

By now, we had reached the hotel, which stood shining in the warmth, the sunbeams glinting in the red awning.

'I understand your excitement,' continued the detective. 'But you will not find out until tonight.'

I asked him to give me a more precise time.

He gave it some thought, calculated.

'Ten o'clock,' he said.

'Very well. So shall I come and find you at the hotel?'

'Yes.'

I was about to go, but when Asbjørn Krag started to laugh, I stayed a while longer.

'You are remarkably incurious,' he said.

I shook my head. I didn't understand what he was talking about.

'I was expecting you to ask me why you should come at precisely ten o'clock.'

'I am sure you have your reasons.'

'Yes, of course. I have a very particular reason. At ten o'clock it will begin to get dark.'

'Is the darkness necessary?'

'Absolutely necessary.'

'Well, then, I shall come at ten o'clock.'

I walked away from him but had only gone a few paces when he called my name.

'Listen, though,' he said. 'It is possible you may not find me at the hotel.'

'Should I wait for you, then?'

'No, in that case you should go to a place where I will be waiting for you if I am not at the hotel.'

'Where?'

Asbjørn Krag pointed down towards the sea.

'Do you see that large stand of trees down there?'

'Yes.'

'You will find me down there. But go to the hotel first.'

'Down there, where the hilltop road begins?' I murmured.

'Yes,' he replied.

Then he nodded a farewell and walked away from me quickly. I stood still for a while, looking after him. He waded through the violet clover meadows that separated the hotel from the road. He stepped onto the veranda and threw open the glass doors noisily. I heard him send a loud, happy greeting into the room.

The warm day rolled slowly around. I lay in the rocking chair in my cabin and let the hours drift past me. For a long time, the creaking of the chair was the only sound I heard. There was no wind and the immense warmth struck my cabin from all sides, forcing its way in through the open window and filling the room. My papers lay in the baking sun, growing warm and brittle as if they were being dried in front of a stove. I sat with my face turned to the window and its view out over the sea, which filled my window, bright blue. The heavy green foliage and the blue sea were framed by the window like the beautiful colours in a painting. Now and then, a leaf dipped beneath the weight of an insect; now and then a white wing glinted behind the leaf – a sail gliding across the sea. At last, I heard a sound: the delicate voices of small children poking around in the sand nearby and playing with a tin can. Glittering bluebottles flashed through the air, landing on the walls like buzzing projectiles.

But gradually the heat in the room became too oppressive. I went outside and lay on the grass, hands behind my neck. I looked at the sky and tried to encompass larger and larger stretches of it within my gaze. Any eyes that could encompass the entire firmament, I thought, must surely experience the immensity of beauty as an eternal revelation. Light, white cloudlets thronged about the eye of the sun like wings of smoke from a glowing cigarette; down on the horizon fluttered a white-robed army; then fluttered no more. Now there was no longer any movement in the sky: the clouds lay motionless, resting on the air. Above them, the bright blue infinity shone up towards heights no human soul could ever reach. What a vault it formed above the earth! And the rest – how sickly, dark and wretched the whole earth seemed by comparison… The hilltops rose up from the earth like sharply etched shadows – and on the highest peak a fir tree stood with shining trunk and dipped its canopy into the light.

I realised this was one of the summer's last days of victorious might. Dusk fell as soon as the chariot of the sun had rolled down beneath the horizon. Autumn roamed abroad after dark with its long, chilly fingers; the nights were beginning to grow cold. The sight of summer vanishing always gives you the feeling that it will never come again, and you want to enjoy its last days to the fullest possible measure. When the shadows stole into my room, the foliage swirled and swayed in the evening wind and the sea faded to grey, a leaden sorrow came upon me; I felt a quiver in my heart, a fleeting sense of life's end.

How slowly the hours passed after seven o'clock. I shut the windows and marvelled at the bloody tint of the glass. It was the reflection of the sunset. As it sank, the sun dragged a fan of clouds down with it beneath the sea, rust brown in colour, that spiteful hue of autumn. The colour was cast back by reflections in the air, and seeped through the glass of my window. I touched the pane and marvelled again as my fingers, too, grew bloody.

Then came dusk. The gloom slowly filled up the corners, grew ever denser, then spread further and further out. The gilded frames on the walls glinted for a while in the feeble gleam of light from the windows, and for a long time, the round disc of the clock hung there, like a clouded white eye upon the wall. But towards ten o'clock, the last memory of day vanished. The room grew quite dark, and only around the window was there still a dappled, misty light, which grew ever more grey and blind.

In the preceding hour, I had sat and thought about what I should do next. I knew something decisive would happen in the course of the night, and I had the distinct impression that this was the last day I would spend here. At any rate, I could no longer bear to endure the nerve-shattering events down here.

I was no longer afraid. Not in the least. I no longer feared the face with its awful mouth and chalk-white brow, for now I understood how everything fitted together.

I now took a series of precautions that may seem remarkable, but whose explanation lies in what happened next.

I left my cabin at half-past nine. At first I put on my light topcoat, but then I changed my mind and left it behind. Instead, I buttoned my jacket tightly around me. I did not want anything to restrict my movements.

Before I left, I hastily loaded my revolver, and stuck it in my right-hand pocket, so that I could reach it quickly. But when I noticed that it made the pocket bulge suspiciously, I switched the revolver to my inside pocket instead. Now nobody could guess it was there.

I was already a few paces away from the cabin when something struck me. I turned back again and looked over my papers, which lay on the table. They seemed too orderly. I pushed the papers around a bit, wrote a few lines on a monograph I had been working on lately and generally tried to give the impression that I had interrupted my work and left the cabin quite by chance.

Then at last I left for good. I kept a constant eye on the clock, because I wanted to be punctual. It was 9.40 when I stepped over the threshold of the country store.

There were five people in the shop: behind the counter stood the storekeeper himself, who was measuring some striped fabric, and his daughter, who was weighing syrup in a can. In front of the counter stood the storekeeper's brother, a fisherman, hands in pocket and pipe hanging slackly from his mouth. Of customers were there only two: an old lady, who stood packing some full bags into a basket, and a little lad who stood there, barefoot and freezing, a tin pail in one hand and a battered blue passbook in the other.

I went into the shop, making noise enough to ensure that everybody would notice my arrival. I greeted the storekeeper's brother, whom I knew from previous visits. I quickly told him that I was thinking of taking a longish fishing trip to Hvassodden, a few miles distant. I planned to row from here in half an hour, sleep for an hour at the fisherman's cabin out on the headland and then set out at around four o'clock.

'Ah, yes, that's a fine fishing trip,' said the man. 'Will you row out there alone?'

'No, I was thinking of taking somebody from the hotel with me.'

'Ah, is that so? Well, it's a tough spot of rowing, after all.'

'Oh, I'll probably manage,' I replied, smiling and flexing my arms.

The man nodded. 'You look pretty strong,' he said.

'Yes, thank goodness,' I replied, my tone more heartfelt than I'd intended.

Then I turned to the storekeeper.

I bought various items of fishing equipment – hooks and a couple of lines. The ones I had were not good enough, I said. The storekeeper gave me some useful advice about fishing, as well as telling me what bait I should use and where I should drop anchor.

In the end, I asked if I could borrow his boat, and after some consideration of the matter, he agreed.

'I shall come and pick the boat up in half an hour or so, then,' I said. 'I may have a friend from the hotel with me, or perhaps I shall have to go out on my own. Whatever happens, I'll most certainly go – I'm terribly keen on taking this fishing trip.'

I had my purchases packaged up, the storekeeper and his brother wished me happy fishing and then I strolled up to the hotel.

Light was shining in all the windows, including Asbjørn Krag's. That was a disappointment. I had certainly not expected him to be there. I firmly believed he had some reason for arranging to meet me down where the hilltop road began. If, after all, I met him here at the hotel, I would have to change my course of action. But come hell or high water, I had reached a decision now, and I would go through with it.

Down in the dining room, I met a couple of guests and asked

if they wanted to join me on my fishing trip. But nobody seemed particularly keen – I had also made it clear that a lot of rowing would be involved. I mentioned the precise time I planned to leave. In half an hour, I said. I would be taking the storekeeper's boat. No, nobody seemed to want to come with me.

Next I walked along the corridor to Asbjørn Krag's room.

At ten o'clock precisely I knocked on his door. Nobody answered. I knocked again, but when there was still no reply, I walked quickly into the room.

It was empty, but the lamp was burning on the table.

I knew that Asbjørn Krag always took care to lock his room. So he could not be far away.

I waited by the door for several minutes. But nobody came, and I could not hear any footsteps. Absolute silence surrounded me.

I thought it peculiar. The door open and the lamp burning on the table… The detective, normally precision personified, knew I would be here at the agreed time – ten o'clock on the dot. I realised he had secrets and that he would not want a stranger to go through his papers under any circumstance – perhaps especially not me. Why, then, was he not more cautious?

I opened the door into the corridor. Asbjørn Krag's room lay roughly halfway along the passage. Whichever direction anyone approached it from, I would be able to hear their footsteps before they actually reached the detective's door. I shut myself into the room again and stood still, listening. Not a sound. I walked over to the detective's desk, where a great many papers were arranged in bundles.

On top of the table closest to the window lay an oval toilet mirror in a silver-plated frame. A number of small items were scattered around this mirror, including several tubes of cosmetics. When I saw these items, I gave a start.

But I also saw something else.

Beside the mirror, in a carved ash wood frame, was a photograph.

It was a photograph of the murdered man, Forestry Inspector Blinde. It was a splendid photograph, which must have been taken shortly before he died.

I picked it up and stared at it for a long time. The same feeling that had seized me on seeing the face behind the green windowpane – I felt a waft of it now. But it lasted only a second and then I was calm again. I realised that Asbjørn Krag had left his door open on purpose. He wanted me to go into the room and see what was lying on the table.

But it didn't surprise me as much as he had, perhaps, reckoned it would. The sight of the photograph, the mirror and these items did not fray my nerves again as the sight of the face behind the windowpane had. Now at least I knew that it was all true. I now had irrefutable knowledge that everything I had only surmised up until now was really true.

I stood and considered what action I should take. I knew that Asbjørn Krag was waiting for me at this very moment in the coal-black darkness beneath the old trees, down there by the sea. In a short while, I would meet him and hear his jarring little laugh.

Now I did something that was quite consistent with my earlier measures. Now, too, I was acting on the basis of a particular thought and was following a plan.

I took a sheet of white paper and placed it on the table before me. I would write to him. There were a great many pencils and a single pen on a pen rack. There was no inkwell. It was a fountain pen. I used it to write on the paper – marvelling at the straight, firm letters I managed to produce.

Dear Krag

I dropped in to look for you this evening at half-past ten [the time was not yet more than 10.10] and take you on a fishing trip to Hvassodden. I shall be leaving at eleven o'clock from the jetty by the country store. If you see this note before then and feel like a trip, do come along.

I signed my name underneath and carefully placed the fountain pen back in the pen rack.

Then I hastily began to rifle through the detective's papers.

He had written a great deal about all manner of different things; but I did not find a single word written about the forestry inspector's death. Or about Dr Brahms's flying machine.

But the minutes were rushing swiftly by. The time had come to leave.

I walked through the dining room, where a couple of guests were still sitting. I whistled a merry tune and rattled my fishing equipment so that everyone would see.

'Will nobody come with me, then?' I asked, one last time.

'No, no,' came the reply.

I came out onto the road and marvelled at how calm I felt.

Remembering what the storekeeper's brother had said about my strength, I stretched out my arms and felt my muscles tense beneath my clothing. I knew what lay ahead.

I walked down the road slowly, hoping to meet one of the guests or a local. I wanted to be seen one more time. In this, too, I was successful. I met the fisherman with the straw hat.

I had not seen this man since that sinister night after the forestry inspector was killed. Now, when he recognised me in the darkness, he slowed his pace and greeted me tentatively. He clearly wished to exchange some words with me, it seemed. I stopped and held out a hand.

'Out so late?' I began.

'Oh, it's only just past ten,' he answered. 'I've been down to the store. I hear you're off fishing.'

I was inordinately pleased that people had already begun to talk about my fishing trip.

'I thought you'd already left,' continued the man. 'Did you find anybody to keep you company?'

'No. I had thought I might take the detective, but he's nowhere to be found. Could you tell him if you meet him that I shall be setting off in a quarter of an hour?'

'Yes, I'll do that.'

The man stood there, rocking back and forth. It was clear he had something on his mind.

In the end, he came out with it: 'Have you seen the iron chariot?'

'Yes,' I replied laughing. 'That is how all ghost stories end, my dear chap. The iron chariot simply doesn't exist. It is a flying machine.'

The man chewed this over. It seemed he still believed in the iron chariot.

'I heard it before,' he said. 'I heard it four years ago.'

'But it turned out that old Gjærnæs didn't die then after all.'

'No, no. But I heard the chariot.'

He remained firm in his superstition and went on his way deeply disappointed that I had now fallen by the wayside.

Without any difficulty I found my way to the boat, which was moored by the jetty. I put my fishing equipment in the aft bulkhead and cast off, making as much noise as I possibly could. I saw the light in one of the storekeeper's windows grow suddenly brighter, then dim again a little while later. I knew what that meant. The storekeeper had opened the window to hear who was messing about with the boats. He had realised it

163

was me and shut the window again.

In other words, everything was going splendidly. It was now a quarter past ten, and the storekeeper had heard me setting off from the jetty.

The only thing now troubling me was the stillness of the night. I would rather have had wind and crashing waves, which could have muffled the noise of my rowing. On the other hand, the darkness helped me. Just a few yards away from land I could no longer see the houses. They vanished into the dense darkness. A few golden spots of light twinkled in the gloom around me, and their reflections floated in long ribbons across the sea. I rowed in the darkest shadows. For the sea was divided into black and grey in the most peculiar fashion. Across long stretches, the surface of the water was tinged a strange pale grey. I could not understand where this light was coming from, but I took good care not to row into these patches of oxidised silver, because I knew that both the boat and I would then be clearly framed in coal-black silhouette.

As I approached the open sea, I felt a gust from the vast plains upon the back of my neck. The boat crept over the backs of the long swells. Now, I should have rowed alongside the low land to the left in order to reach the fishing grounds. But instead, I rowed to the right, in towards the sheer rock face, and felt myself vanish into a vast, shadowy pit. Now I would not have wished to meet another soul, not for anything in the world. I knew that the fishermen often travelled this way, and I hauled on my oars in order to reach my destination quickly and unseen. I strained with all my might and felt the oars shudder as their quivering blades thrust aside the sea.

At last, my boat glided in towards some black posts and I had to row back vigorously to avoid crashing into the jetty. Even so, there was a thump that made the rivets shriek. I sat for a while and listened, but heard no noise; there seemed to be nobody nearby.

I moored the boat alongside some other vessels that lay about me in the darkness, still and shadowy. My arrival had set the sea in gentle motion, rocking the shadows and setting off a faint and feeble gurgling between the piles of the jetty. I climbed on to the jetty and fastened the painter in such a way that I could loosen it again in an instant.

I looked around me. Over there, against the ash-grey sky, stood the mighty, coal-black silhouettes of the trees. In this marvellous shadow, I would meet the man and learn the murderer's name.

It must have been half-past ten by now; in an hour, perhaps even as little as a half that time, it would all be over. I did not feel the slightest trace of tension or unease, but was driven on by the wild urging of my will. Nothing in the world could stop me now. I remember noting, with inner joy, how prudent my actions were in those moments; how alert I was to the unexpected; how wide-open and quivering my senses were as they sought out sights and sounds. My brain was cold and clear.

I walked across the jetty, whose planks creaked faintly beneath my tread. This irritated me, and I tried to walk noiselessly. I reached dry land and found myself on a lawn. Here I stood for a while and listened. Not a sound.

Now, where was the road? Above all, I must not meet anybody. I tried to orientate myself. Over there, a glimpse of a little house, looming out of the darkness like a grey slab; opposite it, a large, knotty mass, which must be a bigger house surrounded by fruit trees; and to my right, a bathing hut I was already familiar with. It was made from an old pilothouse, which had simply been lifted off the deck of a boat and set down on the surface of the water, where it was kept afloat with the aid of empty barrels. As

165

soon as I recognised it, it also became clear to me what I had to do. I had bathed from that spot several times, and knew that a little path led from the pilothouse to the bare rocks directly below the hilltop path, which were always baked by the sun. From there, it was not far to the vast shadow.

I stole along the path; I was slightly troubled by the pebbles and gravel that crunched beneath my tread, but I walked on, cautious and light-footed, slunk onwards on delicate wolf claws. When I reached the bare rocks, I crouched down and crept forward on all fours, so that my black shadow would not be visible against the faintly luminous horizon, out where the open sea began.

At last I reached the rocky hillside, which sloped up towards the path. I seized hold of a willow bush, wet with dew down to the roots. I swung myself up, grasped a tree trunk, then another willow bush, and flung my arms at last around a boulder, which almost came loose and sent me sliding down to the sea. I used my knees to halt my descent, and felt them being scraped and growing sticky with seeping blood. But I didn't have far to go now before I would reach the path. I released the boulder from my embrace; it lay still. To my delight, I managed to claw my fingers fast in some raspberry bushes. Now I had climbed all the way up to the nearest guard stone; I gripped its sharp edge and clung to it so firmly that my nails were bent backwards. Just one small swing of my body and I would be up... Hello?

I heard footsteps.

Footsteps. My heart was like a tree set trembling by a passing breeze. Never before had I felt a fear so alert and sentient: it seemed to slacken the strength of my muscles and loosen my tensed sinews. I heard footsteps there in the darkness, rapid footsteps walking along the road. Straight ahead of me was a vast, wet rock face, dripping with water; a huge, coal-black maw of darkness that stifled every glint of light. And through the sharp-etched shadow of this rock face, up on the road, walked the footsteps. I couldn't catch even a glimpse of the walker. Now he came closer, his steps strangely measured, his soles striking sharply against the surface of the road. As the footsteps passed by me, I thought I could tell from the sound that there must be two people walking. Further up, the road curved around the rock face and I could see its flat bend against the horizon, against the grey sky. I stared eagerly at this spot because I knew that the walkers must come into view there.

And right away, I saw the two of them (for there were two). First I saw their hats, and then their bodies. They were not speaking, but walked along the road together in perfect time, like two black soldiers. Their trousers were gathered at their ankles. It was the two cyclists who had arrived on the steamer that morning. Nobody had seen them all the livelong day and nobody knew where they were. I found it strange that they had suddenly appeared like this. And the way they walked, silent and poker-straight, they looked to me like two dead men. They vanished quickly behind the rock face, which at once smothered the sound of their footsteps.

I had to lie still for a while to collect myself and conquer my fear, but I quickly grew calmer, because they had not seen me; I waited for a minute, then rapidly swung myself up onto the road, and at once slid in towards the rock face, into the great darkness beneath the hilltop.

I had successfully managed to avoid the road between the houses, where I knew that I might risk meeting people at any moment. Now it was only a few paces down to the big trees where Asbjørn Krag was waiting for me. I walked down there quietly, my footsteps making not the slightest sound – never before had I made such desperate efforts to walk noiselessly.

And at last I stood beneath the trees. But where was the man? I felt an awful, crushing silence all around me. I couldn't see a thing because of the darkness, nor was there any sound to be heard either near or far. Not even the branches were swaying, and the great canopies of the trees seemed stiff and charred. I felt as if I were in a burial chamber.

But at last I saw the face.

Suddenly it was there, right before my own: the detective's bloodless, bony face, with its jutting cheekbones and its thin lips. The gleam of his eyes flickered in the glass of his pince-nez. He had appeared all at once from God knows where; he had emerged from the darkness itself. Had he followed me perhaps? The thought made me shudder.

I suddenly found I had no desire to say anything. I was uncertain of my own voice. At this precise moment, I was fairly calm, but God knows I realised the agitation lay in wait for me, ready to spring out and overwhelm me. It felt as if an eternity passed before I heard the detective's voice.

At last he said: 'I have been waiting a long time.'

'I went to look for you at the hotel,' I replied. 'And I waited several minutes in your room.'

'Let us leave.'

The detective took a few steps towards the hilltop road. I followed him, cautious as before. He guessed at once what I was thinking.

'No need to go so carefully,' he said. 'There's nobody nearby.'

'Are you certain of it?'

'Yes, I am. I have been standing here for a long time.'

When we entered the deep shadow beneath the cliff face, the detective stopped. There was a distinct ring of scorn in his voice as he asked: 'Does it not strike you as odd, all things considered, that we should observe such secrecy?'

The question confused me. My own motives made this secrecy entirely reasonable – indeed necessary. But it had never once crossed my mind that Asbjørn Krag might also have his reasons for behaving discreetly, for ensuring that nobody should see him. He wanted to tell me the murderer's name – that was all. Why hadn't he told me earlier in the evening? Why couldn't he tell me now, at this very moment? Only now did it dawn on me how remarkable his behaviour had been this evening, and a suspicion coursed through me, froze me with terror. Did he know what I had in mind? Had he quietly encouraged me to it – was he such a devil that he had even counted on it?

My brain spawned all these thoughts in a second. I muttered an indistinct reply to the detective's question.

'I have given up,' I said. 'I have given up marvelling at your conduct.'

'But why are you so secretive yourself? Why do you creep around like a thief in the night?'

'I thought it was necessary to act with caution,' I said. 'The murderer has not yet been caught.'

The detective laughed at that. He turned his face away and laughed. His laughter was whinnying, scornful. It seemed to emerge from the very darkness.

Then he took me by the arm in a friendly fashion and walked slowly up the road. We were rapidly approaching the spot where the abrupt precipice plunged several hundred feet straight into the sea.

'Poor fellow,' he murmured compassionately. 'You are so terribly nervy and frightened. You need a rest and a change of air, and you shall have both when this case has been brought to a successful conclusion.'

'Shouldn't you hurry up?' I asked.

We were now at the top. Here, where it was supposed to

happen. We both stopped and stared down into the dark, bottomless chasm, which cast a gust of cold air up towards us.

'Indeed. And now you will hear what I have to tell you,' he replied. 'But first, I must ask you a few questions. Will you be able to answer me?'

'Why should I not be able to answer?'

'Your voice is as hoarse and unsteady as a drunkard's. But it is probably just emotion again, or perhaps the sinister atmosphere has got the better of you once more. So you have been into my room tonight?'

'Yes.'

'Weren't you surprised to find the door open?'

'Of course.'

'But I can tell you that there was a purpose to it.'

'I can well believe that. You are usually so careful to keep it locked, after all.'

The detective laughed again.

'I admire you,' he said. 'I can tell you are striving to speak carefully. You certainly do have an impressive presence of mind. So can you tell me what my purpose was?'

'No.'

'Then I shall tell you. I wanted you to see my room.'

'Me?'

'Aha. Now your voice is distant and hoarse again. Didn't you see my desk?'

'Yes.'

'What did you find there?'

'Suffice it to say that I found it.'

'Ho ho! You don't want to say it straight out. You found the tubes of cosmetics, didn't you?'

'Yes.'

'And the wig and false beard?'

'Yes. I am well aware, Mr Detective, that you are the one who has been going about disguised as the ghost of the murdered forestry inspector.'

'No doubt you have discovered the reason for it as well?'

'You are always so mysterious. I don't entirely understand you.'

The detective laid a hand upon my shoulder.

'Hullo?' he said. 'I think I can hear...'

We both listened intently.

Deep down, from the ocean, we heard the creaking of oarlocks. A boat was being rowed past, down there beneath the darkness. The sound rose up as if through a funnel. We heard faint voices too – individual, disconnected words, which sounded strangely distant and frail.

'...better in this kind of weather, though...'

We heard no more: the rest was swallowed up by the darkness and the abyss.

'Deep, deep down,' murmured the detective. When he had listened for a while without hearing any more, he continued: 'As I told you before, my dear fellow, I have worked on this sinister case in a thoroughly unorthodox fashion. It was clear to me at once that the forestry inspector must have been murdered. Killed by a man in a fit of rage. It was certainly no premeditated murder. I thought at once of jealousy. When I saw the murdered man's smile, still triumphant even in death, I thought: if he smiled like that at his rival, it might explain why he was instantly struck down. Now, I saw at once that there could hardly be any question of procuring evidence. One might well come close to having a suspicion, but tangible evidence would be impossible to obtain. The crime was too random, too sudden, involved too little premeditation. So I had no choice but to conduct my work in a way that differed greatly from my normal approach.

Let me give you a little example of this, my dear fellow. Two years ago, a rich Englishman vanished mysteriously on the Riviera. Investigations confirmed that it was a case of murder with intent to rob. But the murderer was nowhere to be found and there were no descriptions of him. So what does the clever little French detective in charge of the investigation do? Why, he plays the murdered man. He disguises himself exactly like him, dresses exactly like him and goes on a tour of all the European capitals. He walks along all the most frequented streets and alleys. At last, in St. Petersburg, the thing he has hoped for happens. A man stops in terror at the sight of him. It is the murderer, who believes the victim's ghost has suddenly appeared before him; he flees, deathly pale and petrified. The next moment, he is caught.

'And there, my dear fellow, you have my method. It is only slightly different. I was nursing a particular suspicion. I understood, because I could see more clearly than the others, that only one person could possibly have been the forestry inspector's murderer. And from that very moment, I have pursued this person. The fact that my work was slowed by extraneous factors such as the flying machine and old Gjærnæs's death was neither here nor there.

'Since I lacked any proof, I had to make the individual give himself away. I exploited fear, using it in a way it may never before have been used by any other detective. If I have been cruel, I apologise for it, but what I said the other day is true: I am a poet of fear. And I made him give himself away... Do I really need to tell you who the murderer is?'

The detective's hand lay heavy on my shoulder. He must surely have been able to feel how my body heaved with the beating of my heart.

I heard my voice say – in an odd indistinct tone, 'No, you

certainly do not.'

'No,' said Asbjørn Krag, with a laugh. 'For of course the murderer is you. I realised it from the first instant. From the first time I heard how you stood beneath the trees and watched the forestry inspector, your rival for the affections of Miss Hilde, come out of her apartment. When you walked off across the plain, you were probably no more than deeply unhappy. You had no thought of killing him, although the fact of being turned away from the farm felt like a scorching pain. You misunderstood the reason entirely. But when you caught up with the forestry inspector and he doffed his hat and greeted you – maliciously, triumphantly – you raised your cane at once, your splendid ivory-headed cane, and struck him. Even then, you had no thought of actually killing him, but the misfortune had already occurred: you struck him on the back of the head and he died instantly.'

Asbjørn Krag broke off.

His words streamed past me. I knew what he was saying, but I could not distinguish the words. His deep, grave voice boomed in my ear with a sorrowful ring, like the clash of muted cymbals in a funeral march. I found myself listening out for the splash of oars down in the abyss. They sounded further off now. The boat had glided by. The time was approaching.

Asbjørn Krag continued. 'If I have been cruel to you, I beg your pardon. But I had to act as I have done. There was no other way. I began by speaking to you, and then confused you with my behaviour. And then, at last, I made the dead man appear at your window at night. If you think back, all my behaviour towards you – all my words, my stories, my concealed and unhidden courses of action – were nothing but a chain, an unbroken and cleverly plaited rope that led straight to my goal. With every passing day, I saw you become more and more nervous and desperate. In the end, perhaps you suspected how things actually fitted together. Remember the revolver. You tried to shoot the ghost, didn't you? But I had removed the bullets while I sat admiring your splendid weapon an hour before. That's when you became convinced, isn't it? I could see it the following day. And at last you gave yourself away.'

'I have most certainly not given myself away,' I whispered.

'Oh, but you have. And now I would advise you to confess…'

'Never.'

The detective was walking ahead of me. Now he stood between me and the abyss. He was tempting fate.

'Here we stand now, face to face,' he said. 'Do you really intend to continue denying it?'

'I am not denying it,' I cried, wildly. 'But there is no proof and you shall never have any.'

'Murderer!' he said.

And now the time had come. Now I would act, as I had been planning to the whole evening.

I hurled myself at him and seized him in my strong, sinewy arms.

An instant of shining joy flowed through me.

I felt my powers burgeon, and in the next second I would have cast him down into the abyss. Krag – the only person who knew.

But at just that crucial moment, I found myself seized by many arms. I heard a ringing metallic sound, and suddenly found that my hands were caught behind my back in a vice.

And now it was as if a mist descended upon my mind. I had a flashing glimpse of blinding light. And in that gleam of light, I saw two more figures: the black soldiers, the cyclists. I heard Asbjørn Krag thank them for their speedy action and issue them with orders. Presently, I realised the detective was addressing me.

'At last you have given yourself away,' he said. 'I was obliged to stage another coup de théâtre – and all the while, you thought you would be able to kill me! I have been following you the whole night. Your manoeuvre with the fishing trip was intended to give yourself an alibi if anybody should find my mutilated body. But instead, my dear fellow, you fitted right in with my calculations. For you see I intended this attempted murder to take place. That is precisely why I have repeatedly talked about this dangerous spot. And it worked, my dear fellow, it worked perfectly; as smoothly as the lock on those handcuffs.'

I heard the detective's voice drift further and further away until it vanished into the darkness. And then the smothering silence closed over my mind.

It is a strange feeling, to sit here in this cell and leaf through these papers. The first pages are written in a hasty, uneven hand. The letters are crooked and many of the words are quite illegible. But gradually, the writing becomes calmer, as if I myself have become calmer during the time I have been busy on this account.

The fact is, I now have the most marvellous feeling of peace and certainty; I am in prison, I no longer have any will, nor any cares.

Autumn has come now, and the mornings are cold until the heating system manages to knock some warmth into the different floors of the building. My dreams and my imaginative life are greatly taken up with images of autumn. I seem to see the world outside – leafless trees, their branches bristling like black-burnt fingers. The sky is neither grey nor blue; it has no colour at all, and does not reflect the earth, but lies low upon the lands; it exudes a bitter chill, as if from some hideous, evil entity. The frost has already breathed upon the cast iron of the church bells; I hear it in their muffled chime.

I can sit here for hours on end, staring straight ahead. I feel as if I am drifting further and further away from mankind, and sailing out towards infinity, towards another existence. Perhaps the knowledge of all the prison years that lie ahead is what turns my thoughts so frequently towards eternity. I have a sense that eternity is a thing of light: a strange and marvellous light that shines far out upon a vast and desolate sea.

I have become fond of my cell. It is my pilothouse, and in it I shall take a long journey. I have cast off from humanity. The noise and voices still buzz in my mind like the slow wash of the tide upon the shore; but they sound ever more distant – and soon I shall travel, surrounded by stillness and silence, into those many years.

END